D0886714

WITHDRAWN

Mark Twain
TALES *of* MYSTERY

IDW

Written by Mark Twain
Cover and Illustration by Menton3
Edited by Justin Eisinger and Alonzo Simon
Editorial Assistance by Leslie Manes
Book Design: Rich Sheinaus

Ted Adams, CEO & Publisher
Greg Goldstein, Chief Operating Officer
Robbie Robbins, EVP/Sr. Graphic Artist
Chris Ryall, Chief Creative Officer/Editor-In-Chief
Matthew Ruzicka, CPA, Chief Financial Officer
Alan Payne, VP of Sales

WWW.IDWPUBLISHING.COM

ISBN: 978-1-61377-124-2   15 14 13 12   1 2 3 4

MARK TWAIN'S TALES OF MYSTERY. JANUARY 2012. FIRST PRINTING. © 2012 Idea and Design Works, LLC. The IDW logo is registered in the U.S. Patent and Trademark Office. IDW Publishing, a division of Idea and Design Works, LLC. Editorial offices: 5080 Santa Fe St., San Diego, CA 92109. Any similarities to persons living or dead are purely coincidental. With the exception of artwork used for review purposes, none of the contents of this publication may be reprinted without the permission of Idea and Design Works, LLC. Printed in Korea. IDW Publishing does not read or accept unsolicited submissions of ideas, stories, or artwork.

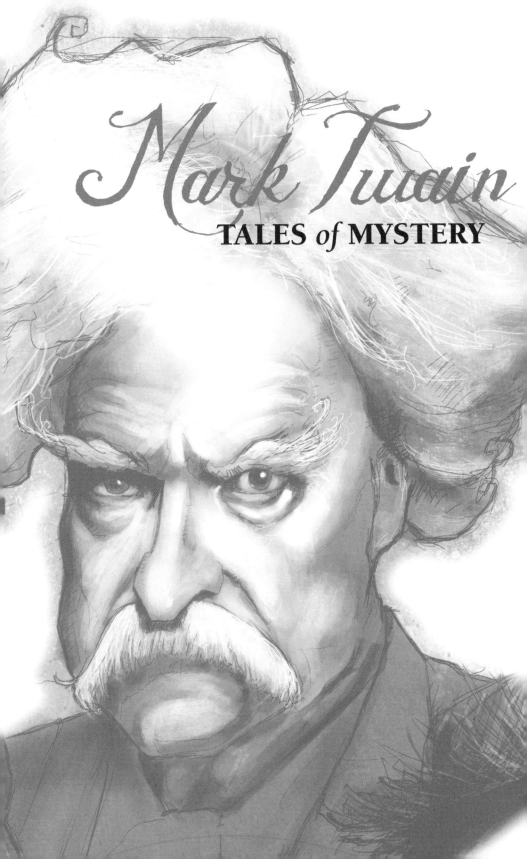

Mark Twain
TALES of MYSTERY

Mark Twain
TALES *of* MYSTERY

TABLE *of* CONTENTS

Tom Sawyer Detective

CHAPTER I – An Invitation for Tom and Huck

[Note: *Strange as the incidents of this story are, they are not inventions, but facts — even to the public confession of the accused. I take them from an old-time Swedish criminal trial, change the actors, and transfer the scenes to America. I have added some details, but only a couple of them are important ones.* — M. T.]

WELL, IT WAS THE NEXT SPRING after me and Tom Sawyer set our old nigger Jim free, the time he was chained up for a runaway slave down there on Tom's uncle Silas's farm in Arkansaw. The frost was working out of the ground, and out of the air, too, and it was getting closer and closer onto barefoot time every day; and next it would be marble time, and next mumbletypeg, and next tops and hoops, and next kites, and then right away it would be summer and going in a-swimming. It just makes a boy homesick to look ahead like that and see how far off summer is. Yes, and it sets him to sighing and saddening around, and there's something the matter with him, he don't know what. But anyway, he gets out by himself and mopes and thinks; and mostly he hunts for a lonesome place high up on the hill in the edge of the woods, and sets there and looks away off on the big Mississippi down there a-reaching miles and miles around the points where the timber looks smoky and dim it's so far off and still, and everything's so solemn it seems like everybody you've loved is dead and gone, and you 'most wish you was dead and gone too, and done with it all.

Don't you know what that is? It's spring fever. That is what the name of it is. And when you've got it, you want — oh, you don't quite know what it is you DO want, but it just fairly makes your heart ache, you want it so! It seems to you that mainly what you want is to get away; get away from the same old tedious things you're so used to seeing and so tired of, and set something new. That is the idea; you want to go and be a wanderer; you want to go wandering far away to strange countries where everything is mysterious and wonderful and romantic. And if you can't do that, you'll put up with considerable less; you'll go anywhere you CAN go, just so as to get away, and be thankful of the chance, too.

Well, me and Tom Sawyer had the spring fever, and had it bad, too; but it warn't any use to think about Tom trying to get away, because, as he said, his Aunt Polly wouldn't let him quit school and go traipsing off somers wasting time; so we was pretty blue. We was setting on the front steps one day about sundown talking this way, when out comes his aunt Polly with a letter in her hand and says:

"Tom, I reckon you've got to pack up and go down to Arkansaw — your aunt Sally wants you."

I 'most jumped out of my skin for joy. I reckoned Tom would fly at his aunt and hug her head off; but if you believe me he set there like a rock, and never said a word. It made me fit to cry to see him act so foolish, with such a noble chance as this opening up. Why, we might lose it if he didn't speak up and show he was thankful and grateful. But he set there and studied and studied till I was that distressed I didn't know what to do; then he says, very ca'm, and I could a shot him for it:

"Well," he says, "I'm right down sorry, Aunt Polly, but I reckon I got to be excused — for the present."

His aunt Polly was knocked so stupid and so mad at the cold impudence of it that she couldn't say a word for as much as a half a minute, and this gave me a chance to nudge Tom and whisper:

"Ain't you got any sense? Sp'iling such a noble chance as this and throwing it away?"

But he warn't disturbed. He mumbled back:

"Huck Finn, do you want me to let her SEE how bad I want to go? Why, she'd begin to doubt, right away, and imagine a lot of sicknesses and dangers and objections, and first you know she'd take it all back. You lemme alone; I reckon I know how to work her."

Now I never would 'a' thought of that. But he was right. Tom Sawyer was always right — the levelest head I ever see, and always AT himself and ready for anything you might spring on him. By this time his aunt Polly was all straight again, and she let fly. She says:

"You'll be excused! YOU will! Well, I never heard the like of it in all my days! The idea of you talking like that to ME! Now take yourself off and pack your traps; and if I hear another word out of you about what you'll be excused from and what you won't, I lay I'LL excuse you — with a hickory!"

She hit his head a thump with her thimble as we dodged by, and he let on to be whimpering as we struck for the stairs. Up in his room he hugged me, he was so out of his head for gladness because he was going traveling. And he says:

"Before we get away she'll wish she hadn't let me go, but she won't know any way to get around it now. After what she's said, her pride won't let her take it back."

Tom was packed in ten minutes, all except what his aunt and Mary would finish up for him; then we waited ten more for her to get cooled down and sweet and gentle again; for Tom said it took her ten minutes to unruffle in times when half of her feathers was up, but twenty when they was all up, and this was one of the times when they was all up. Then we went down, being in a sweat to know what the letter said.

She was setting there in a brown study, with it laying in her lap. We set down, and she says:

"They're in considerable trouble down there, and they think you and Huck'll be a kind of diversion for them — 'comfort,' they say. Much of that they'll get out of you and Huck Finn, I reckon. There's a neighbor named Brace Dunlap that's been wanting to marry their Benny for three months, and at last they told him point blank and once for all, he COULDN'T; so he has soured on them, and they're worried about it. I reckon he's somebody they think they better be on the good side of, for they've tried to please him by hiring his no-account brother to help on the farm when they can't hardly afford it, and don't want him around anyhow. Who are the Dunlaps?"

"They live about a mile from Uncle Silas's place, Aunt Polly — all the farmers live about a mile apart down there — and Brace Dunlap is a long sight richer than any of the others, and owns a whole grist of niggers. He's a widower, thirty-six years old, without any children, and is proud of his money and overbearing, and everybody is a little afraid of him. I judge he thought he could have any girl he wanted, just for the asking, and it must have set him back a good deal when he found he couldn't get Benny. Why, Benny's only half as old as he is, and just as sweet and lovely as — well, you've seen her. Poor old Uncle Silas — why, it's pitiful, him trying to curry favor that way — so hard pushed and poor, and yet hiring that useless Jubiter Dunlap to please his ornery brother."

"What a name — Jubiter! Where'd he get it?"

"It's only just a nickname. I reckon they've forgot his real name long before this. He's twenty-seven, now, and has had it ever since the first time he ever went in swimming. The school teacher seen a round brown mole the size of a dime on his left leg above his knee, and four little bits of moles around it, when he was naked, and he said it minded him of Jubiter and his moons; and the children thought it was funny, and so they got to calling him Jubiter, and he's Jubiter yet. He's tall, and lazy, and sly, and sneaky, and ruther cowardly, too, but kind of good-natured, and wears long brown hair and no beard, and hasn't got a cent, and Brace boards him for nothing, and gives him his old clothes to wear, and despises him. Jubiter is a twin."

"What's t'other twin like?"

"Just exactly like Jubiter — so they say; used to was, anyway, but he hain't been seen for seven years. He got to robbing when he was nineteen or twenty, and they jailed him; but he broke jail and got away — up North here, somers. They used to hear about him robbing and burglaring now and then, but that was years ago. He's dead, now. At least that's what they say. They don't hear about him any more."

"What was his name?"

"Jake."

There wasn't anything more said for a considerable while; the old lady was thinking. At last she says:

"The thing that is mostly worrying your aunt Sally is the tempers that that man Jubiter gets your uncle into."

Tom was astonished, and so was I. Tom says:

"Tempers? Uncle Silas? Land, you must be joking! I didn't know he HAD any temper."

"Works him up into perfect rages, your aunt Sally says; says he acts as if he would really hit the man, sometimes."

"Aunt Polly, it beats anything I ever heard of. Why, he's just as gentle as mush."

"Well, she's worried, anyway. Says your uncle Silas is like a changed man, on account of all this quarreling. And the neighbors talk about it, and lay all the blame on your uncle, of course, because he's a preacher and hain't got any business to quarrel. Your aunt Sally says he hates to go into the pulpit he's so ashamed; and the people have begun to cool toward him, and he ain't as popular now as he used to was."

"Well, ain't it strange? Why, Aunt Polly, he was always so good and kind and moony and absent-minded and chuckle-headed and lovable — why, he was just an angel! What CAN be the matter of him, do you reckon?"

CHAPTER **II** – Jake Dunlap

W E HAD POWERFUL GOOD LUCK; because we got a chance in a stern-wheeler from away North which was bound for one of them bayous or one-horse rivers away down Louisiana way, and so we could go all the way down the Upper Mississippi and all the way down the Lower Mississippi to that farm in Arkansaw without having to change steamboats at St. Louis; not so very much short of a thousand miles at one pull.

A pretty lonesome boat; there warn't but few passengers, and all old folks, that set around, wide apart, dozing, and was very quiet. We was four days getting out of the "upper river," because we got aground so much. But it warn't dull — couldn't be for boys that was traveling, of course.

From the very start me and Tom allowed that there was somebody sick in the stateroom next to ourn, because the meals was always toted in there by the waiters. By and by we asked about it — Tom did and the waiter said it was a man, but he didn't look sick.

"Well, but AIN'T he sick?"

"I don't know; maybe he is, but 'pears to me he's just letting on."

"What makes you think that?"

"Because if he was sick he would pull his clothes off SOME time or other — don't you reckon he would? Well, this one don't. At least he don't ever pull off his boots, anyway."

"The mischief he don't! Not even when he goes to bed?"

"No."

It was always nuts for Tom Sawyer — a mystery was. If you'd lay out a mystery and a pie before me and him, you wouldn't have to say take your choice; it was a thing that would regulate itself. Because in my nature I have always run to pie, whilst in his nature he has always run to mystery. People are made different. And it is the best way. Tom says to the waiter:

"What's the man's name?"

"Phillips."

"Where'd he come aboard?"

"I think he got aboard at Elexandria, up on the Iowa line."

"What do you reckon he's a-playing?"

"I hain't any notion — I never thought of it."

I says to myself, here's another one that runs to pie.

"Anything peculiar about him? — the way he acts or talks?"

"No — nothing, except he seems so scary, and keeps his doors locked night and day both, and when you knock he won't let you in till he opens the door a crack and sees who it is."

"By jimminy, it's int'resting! I'd like to get a look at him. Say — the next time you're going in there, don't you reckon you could spread the door and — "

"No, indeedy! He's always behind it. He would block that game."

Tom studied over it, and then he says:

"Looky here. You lend me your apern and let me take him his breakfast in the morning. I'll give you a quarter."

The boy was plenty willing enough, if the head steward wouldn't mind. Tom says that's all right, he reckoned he could fix it with the head steward; and he done it. He fixed it so as we could both go in with aperns on and toting vittles.

He didn't sleep much, he was in such a sweat to get in there and find out the mystery about Phillips; and moreover he done a lot of guessing about it all night, which warn't no use, for if you are going to find out the facts of a thing, what's the sense in guessing out what ain't the facts and wasting ammunition? I didn't lose no sleep. I wouldn't give a dern to know what's the matter of Phillips, I says to myself.

Well, in the morning we put on the aperns and got a couple of trays of truck, and Tom he knocked on the door. The man opened it a crack, and then he let us in and shut it quick. By Jackson, when we got a sight of him, we 'most dropped the trays! and Tom says:

"Why, Jubiter Dunlap, where'd YOU come from?"

Well, the man was astonished, of course; and first off he looked like he didn't know whether to be scared, or glad, or both, or which, but finally he settled down to being glad; and then his color come back, though at first his face had turned pretty white. So we got to talking together while he et his breakfast. And he says:

"But I aint Jubiter Dunlap. I'd just as soon tell you who I am, though, if you'll swear to keep mum, for I ain't no Phillips, either."

Tom says:

"We'll keep mum, but there ain't any need to tell who you are if you ain't Jubiter Dunlap."

"Why?"

"Because if you ain't him you're t'other twin, Jake. You're the spit'n image of Jubiter."

"Well, I'm Jake. But looky here, how do you come to know us Dunlaps?"

Tom told about the adventures we'd had down there at his uncle Silas's last summer, and when he see that there warn't anything about his folks — or him either, for that matter — that we didn't know, he opened out and talked perfectly free and candid. He never made any bones about his own case; said he'd been a hard lot, was a hard lot yet, and reckoned he'd be a hard lot plumb to the end. He said of course it was a dangerous life, and — He give a kind of gasp, and set his head like a person that's listening. We didn't say anything, and so it was very still for a second or so, and there warn't no sounds but the screaking of the woodwork and the chug-chugging of the machinery down below.

Then we got him comfortable again, telling him about his people, and how Brace's wife had been dead three years, and Brace wanted to marry Benny and she shook him, and Jubiter was working for Uncle Silas, and him and Uncle Silas quarreling all the time — and then he let go and laughed.

"Land!" he says, "it's like old times to hear all this tittle-tattle, and does me good. It's been seven years and more since I heard any. How do they talk about me these days?"

"Who?"

"The farmers — and the family."

"Why, they don't talk about you at all — at least only just a mention, once in a long time."

"The nation!" he says, surprised; "why is that?"

"Because they think you are dead long ago."

"No! Are you speaking true? — honor bright, now." He jumped up, excited.

"Honor bright. There ain't anybody thinks you are alive."

"Then I'm saved, I'm saved, sure! I'll go home. They'll hide me and save my life. You keep mum. Swear you'll keep mum — swear you'll never, never tell on me. Oh, boys, be good to a poor devil that's being hunted day and night, and dasn't show his face! I've never done you any harm; I'll never do you any, as God is in the heavens; swear you'll be good to me and help me save my life."

We'd a swore it if he'd been a dog; and so we done it. Well, he couldn't love us enough for it or be grateful enough, poor cuss; it was all he could do to keep from hugging us.

We talked along, and he got out a little hand-bag and begun to open it, and told us to turn our backs. We done it, and when he told us to turn again he was perfectly different to what he was before. He had on blue goggles and the naturalest-looking long brown whiskers and mustashes you ever see. His own mother wouldn't 'a' knowed him. He asked us if he looked like his brother Jubiter, now.

"No," Tom said; "there ain't anything left that's like him except the long hair."

"All right, I'll get that cropped close to my head before I get there; then him and Brace will keep my secret, and I'll live with them as being a stranger, and the neighbors won't ever guess me out. What do you think?"

Tom he studied awhile, then he says:

"Well, of course me and Huck are going to keep mum there, but if you don't keep mum yourself there's going to be a little bit of a risk — it ain't much, maybe, but it's a little. I mean, if you talk, won't people notice that your voice is just like Jubiter's; and mightn't it make them think of the twin they reckoned was dead, but maybe after all was hid all this time under another name?"

"By George," he says, "you're a sharp one! You're perfectly right. I've got to play deef and dumb when there's a neighbor around. If I'd a struck for home and forgot that little detail — However, I wasn't striking for home. I was breaking for any place where I could get away from these fellows that are after me; then I was going to put on this disguise and get some different clothes, and — "

He jumped for the outside door and laid his ear against it and listened, pale and kind of panting. Presently he whispers:

"Sounded like cocking a gun! Lord, what a life to lead!"

Then he sunk down in a chair all limp and sick like, and wiped the sweat off of his face.

CHAPTER III – A Diamond Robbery

F ROM THAT TIME OUT, we was with him 'most all the time, and one or
t'other of us slept in his upper berth. He said he had been so lonesome,
and it was such a comfort to him to have company, and somebody to talk to
in his troubles. We was in a sweat to find out what his secret was, but Tom
said the best way was not to seem anxious, then likely he would drop into it
himself in one of his talks, but if we got to asking questions he would get suspicious and shet up his shell. It turned out just so. It warn't no trouble to see
that he WANTED to talk about it, but always along at first he would scare
away from it when he got on the very edge of it, and go to talking about
something else. The way it come about was this: He got to asking us, kind of
indifferent like, about the passengers down on deck. We told him about them.
But he warn't satisfied; we warn't particular enough. He told us to describe
them better. Tom done it. At last, when Tom was describing one of the
roughest and raggedest ones, he gave a shiver and a gasp and says:

"Oh, lordy, that's one of them! They're aboard sure — I just knowed it. I
sort of hoped I had got away, but I never believed it. Go on."

Presently when Tom was describing another mangy, rough deck passenger,
he give that shiver again and says:

"That's him! — that's the other one. If it would only come a good black
stormy night and I could get ashore. You see, they've got spies on me.
They've got a right to come up and buy drinks at the bar yonder forrard,
and they take that chance to bribe somebody to keep watch on me — porter

or boots or somebody. If I was to slip ashore without anybody seeing me, they would know it inside of an hour."

So then he got to wandering along, and pretty soon, sure enough, he was telling! He was poking along through his ups and downs, and when he come to that place he went right along. He says:

"It was a confidence game. We played it on a julery-shop in St. Louis. What we was after was a couple of noble big di'monds as big as hazel-nuts, which everybody was running to see. We was dressed up fine, and we played it on them in broad daylight. We ordered the di'monds sent to the hotel for us to see if we wanted to buy, and when we was examining them we had paste counterfeits all ready, and THEM was the things that went back to the shop when we said the water wasn't quite fine enough for twelve thousand dollars."

"Twelve-thousand-dollars!" Tom says. "Was they really worth all that money, do you reckon?"

"Every cent of it."

"And you fellows got away with them?"

"As easy as nothing. I don't reckon the julery people know they've been robbed yet. But it wouldn't be good sense to stay around St. Louis, of course, so we considered where we'd go. One was for going one way, one another, so we threw up, heads or tails, and the Upper Mississippi won. We done up the di'monds in a paper and put our names on it and put it in the keep of the hotel clerk, and told him not to ever let either of us have it again without the others was on hand to see it done; then we went down town, each by his own self — because I reckon maybe we all had the same notion. I don't know for certain, but I reckon maybe we had."

"What notion?" Tom says.

"To rob the others."

"What — one take everything, after all of you had helped to get it?"

"Cert'nly."

It disgusted Tom Sawyer, and he said it was the orneriest, low-downest thing he ever heard of. But Jake Dunlap said it warn't unusual in the profession. Said when a person was in that line of business he'd got to look out for his own intrust, there warn't nobody else going to do it for him. And then he went on. He says:

"You see, the trouble was, you couldn't divide up two di'monds amongst three. If there'd been three — But never mind about that, there warn't three. I loafed along the back streets studying and studying. And I says to myself, I'll hog them di'monds the first chance I get, and I'll have a disguise all ready, and I'll give the boys the slip, and when I'm safe away I'll put it on, and then let them find me if they can. So I got the false whiskers and the goggles and this countrified suit of clothes, and fetched them along back in a hand-bag; and when I was passing a shop where they sell all sorts of things, I got a glimpse of one of my pals through the window. It was Bud Dixon. I was glad, you bet. I says to myself, I'll see what he buys. So I kept shady, and watched. Now what do you reckon it was he bought?"

"Whiskers?" said I.

"No."

"Goggles?"

"No."

"Oh, keep still, Huck Finn, can't you, you're only just hendering all you can. What WAS it he bought, Jake?"

"You'd never guess in the world. It was only just a screwdriver — just a wee little bit of a screwdriver."

"Well, I declare! What did he want with that?"

"That's what I thought. It was curious. It clean stumped me. I says to myself, what can he want with that thing? Well, when he come out I stood back out of sight, and then tracked him to a second-hand slop-shop and see him buy a red flannel shirt and some old ragged clothes — just the ones he's got on now, as you've described. Then I went down to the wharf and hid my things aboard the up-river boat that we had picked out, and then started back and had another streak of luck. I seen our other pal lay in HIS stock of old rusty second-handers. We got the di'monds and went aboard the boat.

"But now we was up a stump, for we couldn't go to bed. We had to set up and watch one another. Pity, that was; pity to put that kind of a strain on us, because there was bad blood between us from a couple of weeks back, and we was only friends in the way of business. Bad anyway, seeing there was only two di'monds betwixt three men. First we had supper, and then tramped up and down the deck together smoking till most midnight; then we went and set down in my stateroom and locked the doors and looked in the piece of paper to see if the di'monds was all right, then laid it on the lower berth right in full sight; and there we set, and set, and by-and-by it got to be dreadful hard to keep awake. At last Bud Dixon he dropped off. As soon as he was snoring a good regular gait that was likely to last, and had his chin on his breast and looked permanent, Hal Clayton nodded towards the di'monds and then towards the outside door, and I understood. I reached and got the paper, and then we stood up and waited perfectly still; Bud never stirred; I turned the key of the outside door very soft and slow, then turned the knob the same way, and we went tiptoeing out onto the guard, and shut the door very soft and gentle.

"There warn't nobody stirring anywhere, and the boat was slipping along, swift and steady, through the big water in the smoky moonlight. We never said a word, but went straight up onto the hurricane-deck and plumb back aft, and set down on the end of the sky-light. Both of us knowed what that meant, without having to explain to one another. Bud Dixon would wake up and miss the swag, and would come straight for us, for he ain't afeard of anything or anybody, that man ain't. He would come, and we would heave him overboard, or get killed trying. It made me shiver, because I ain't as brave as some people, but if I showed the white feather — well, I knowed better than do that. I kind of hoped the boat would land somers, and we could skip ashore and not have to run the risk of this row, I was so scared of Bud Dixon, but she was an upper-river tub and there warn't no real chance of that.

"Well, the time strung along and along, and that fellow never come! Why, it strung along till dawn begun to break, and still he never come. 'Thunder,' I says, 'what do you make out of this? — ain't it suspicious?' 'Land!' Hal says, 'do you reckon he's playing us? — open the paper!' I done it, and by gracious there warn't anything in it but a couple of little pieces of loaf-sugar! THAT'S the reason he could set there and snooze all night so comfortable. Smart? Well, I reckon! He had had them two papers all fixed and ready, and he had put one of them in place of t'other right under our noses.

"We felt pretty cheap. But the thing to do, straight off, was to make a plan; and we done it. We would do up the paper again, just as it was, and slip in, very elaborate and soft, and lay it on the bunk again, and let on WE didn't know about any trick, and hadn't any idea he was a-laughing at us behind them bogus snores of his'n; and we would stick by him, and the first night we was ashore we would get him drunk and search him, and get the di'monds; and DO for him, too, if it warn't too risky. If we got the swag, we'd GOT to do for him, or he would hunt us down and do for us, sure. But I didn't have no real hope. I knowed we could get him drunk — he was always ready for that — but what's the good of it? You might search him a year and never find — Well, right there I catched my breath and broke off my thought! For an idea went ripping through my head that tore my brains to rags — and land, but I felt gay and good! You see, I had had my boots off, to unswell my feet, and just then I took up one of them to put it on, and I catched a glimpse of the heel-bottom, and it just took my breath away. You remember about that puzzlesome little screwdriver?"

"You bet I do," says Tom, all excited.

"Well, when I catched that glimpse of that boot heel, the idea that went smashing through my head was, I know where he's hid the di'monds! You look at this boot heel, now. See, it's bottomed with a steel plate, and the plate is fastened on with little screws. Now there wasn't a screw about that feller anywhere but in his boot heels; so, if he needed a screwdriver, I reckoned I knowed why."

"Huck, ain't it bully!" says Tom.

"Well, I got my boots on, and we went down and slipped in and laid the paper of sugar on the berth, and sat down soft and sheepish and went to listening to Bud Dixon snore. Hal Clayton dropped off pretty soon, but I didn't; I wasn't ever so wide awake in my life. I was spying out from under the shade of my hat brim, searching the floor for leather. It took me a long time, and I begun to think maybe my guess was wrong, but at last I struck it. It laid over by the bulkhead, and was nearly the color of the carpet. It was a little round plug about as thick as the end of your little finger, and I says to myself there's a di'mond in the nest you've come from. Before long I spied out the plug's mate.

"Think of the smartness and coolness of that blatherskite! He put up that scheme on us and reasoned out what we would do, and we went ahead and done it perfectly exact, like a couple of pudd'nheads. He set there and took his own time to unscrew his heelplates and cut out his plugs and stick in the di'monds and screw on his plates again. He allowed we would steal the bogus swag and wait all night for him to come up and get drownded, and by George it's just what we done! I think it was powerful smart."

"You bet your life it was!" says Tom, just full of admiration.

CHAPTER IV – The Three Sleepers

"WELL, ALL DAY WE WENT THROUGH the humbug of watching one another, and it was pretty sickly business for two of us and hard to act out, I can tell you. About night we landed at one of them little Missouri towns high up toward Iowa, and had supper at the tavern, and got a room upstairs with a cot and a double bed in it, but I dumped my bag under a deal table in the dark hall while we was moving along it to bed, single file, me last, and the landlord in the lead with a tallow candle. We had up a lot of whisky, and went to playing high-low-jack for dimes, and as soon as the whisky begun to take hold of Bud we stopped drinking, but we didn't let him stop. We loaded him till he fell out of his chair and laid there snoring.

"We was ready for business now. I said we better pull our boots off, and his'n too, and not make any noise, then we could pull him and haul him around and ransack him without any trouble. So we done it. I set my boots and Bud's side by side, where they'd be handy. Then we stripped him and searched his seams and his pockets and his socks and the inside of his boots, and everything, and searched his bundle. Never found any di'monds. We found the screwdriver, and Hal says, 'What do you reckon he wanted with that?' I said I didn't know; but when he wasn't looking I hooked it. At last Hal he looked beat and discouraged, and said we'd got to give it up. That was what I was waiting for. I says:

"'There's one place we hain't searched.'

"'What place is that?' he says.

"'His stomach.'

"'By gracious, I never thought of that! NOW we're on the homestretch, to a dead moral certainty. How'll we manage?'

"'Well,' I says, 'just stay by him till I turn out and hunt up a drug store, and I reckon I'll fetch something that'll make them di'monds tired of the company they're keeping.'

"He said that's the ticket, and with him looking straight at me I slid myself into Bud's boots instead of my own, and he never noticed. They was just a shade large for me, but that was considerable better than being too small. I got my bag as I went a-groping through the hall, and in about a minute I was out the back way and stretching up the river road at a five-mile gait.

"And not feeling so very bad, neither — walking on di'monds don't have no such effect. When I had gone fifteen minutes I says to myself, there's more'n a mile behind me, and everything quiet. Another five minutes and I says there's considerable more land behind me now, and there's a man back there that's begun to wonder what's the trouble. Another five and I says to myself he's getting real uneasy — he's walking the floor now. Another five, and I says to myself, there's two mile and a half behind me, and he's AWFUL uneasy — beginning to cuss, I reckon. Pretty soon I says to myself, forty minutes gone — he KNOWS there's something up! Fifty minutes — the truth's a-busting on him now! He is reckoning I found the di'monds whilst we was searching, and shoved them in my pocket and never let on — yes, and he's starting out to hunt for me. He'll hunt for new tracks in the dust, and they'll as likely send him down the river as up.

"Just then I see a man coming down on a mule, and before I thought I jumped into the bush. It was stupid! When he got abreast he stopped and waited a little for me to come out; then he rode on again. But I didn't feel gay any more. I says to myself I've botched my chances by that; I surely have, if he meets up with Hal Clayton.

"Well, about three in the morning I fetched Elexandria and see this stern-

wheeler laying there, and was very glad, because I felt perfectly safe, now, you know. It was just daybreak. I went aboard and got this stateroom and put on these clothes and went up in the pilot-house — to watch, though I didn't reckon there was any need of it. I set there and played with my di'monds and waited and waited for the boat to start, but she didn't. You see, they was mending her machinery, but I didn't know anything about it, not being very much used to steamboats.

"Well, to cut the tale short, we never left there till plumb noon; and long before that I was hid in this stateroom; for before breakfast I see a man coming, away off, that had a gait like Hal Clayton's, and it made me just sick. I says to myself, if he finds out I'm aboard this boat, he's got me like a rat in a trap. All he's got to do is to have me watched, and wait — wait till I slip ashore, thinking he is a thousand miles away, then slip after me and dog me to a good place and make me give up the di'monds, and then he'll — oh, I know what he'll do! Ain't it awful — awful! And now to think the OTHER one's aboard, too! Oh, ain't it hard luck, boys — ain't it hard! But you'll help save me, WON'T you? — Oh, boys, be good to a poor devil that's being hunted to death, and save me — I'll worship the very ground you walk on!"

We turned in and soothed him down and told him we would plan for him and help him, and he needn't be so afeard; and so by and by he got to feeling kind of comfortable again, and unscrewed his heelplates and held up his di'monds this way and that, admiring them and loving them; and when the light struck into them they WAS beautiful, sure; why, they seemed to kind of bust, and snap fire out all around. But all the same I judged he was a fool. If I had been him I would a handed the di'monds to them pals and got them to go ashore and leave me alone. But he was made different. He said it was a whole fortune and he couldn't bear the idea.

Twice we stopped to fix the machinery and laid a good while, once in the night; but it wasn't dark enough, and he was afeard to skip. But the third time we had to fix it there was a better chance. We laid up at a country woodyard about forty mile above Uncle Silas's place a little after one at night, and it was thickening up and going to storm. So Jake he laid for a chance to slide. We begun to take in wood. Pretty soon the rain come a-drenching down, and the wind blowed hard. Of course every boat-hand fixed a gunny sack and put it on like a bonnet, the way they do when they are toting wood, and we got one for Jake, and he slipped down aft with his hand-bag and come tramping forrard just like the rest, and walked ashore with them, and when we see him pass out of the light of the torch-basket and get swallowed up in the dark, we got our breath again and just felt grateful and splendid. But it wasn't for long. Somebody told, I reckon; for in about eight or ten minutes them two pals come tearing forrard as tight as they could jump and darted ashore and was gone. We waited plumb till dawn for them to come back, and kept hoping they would, but they never did. We was awful sorry and low-spirited. All the hope we had was that Jake had got such a start that they couldn't get on his track, and he would get to his brother's and hide there and be safe.

He was going to take the river road, and told us to find out if Brace and Jubiter was to home and no strangers there, and then slip out about sundown and tell him. Said he would wait for us in a little bunch of sycamores right back of Tom's uncle Silas's tobacker field on the river road, a lonesome place.

We set and talked a long time about his chances, and Tom said he was all right if the pals struck up the river instead of down, but it wasn't likely, because maybe they knowed where he was from; more likely they would go right, and dog him all day, him not suspecting, and kill him when it come dark, and take the boots. So we was pretty sorrowful.

CHAPTER V – A Tragedy in the Woods

WE DIDN'T GET DONE TINKERING the machinery till away late in the afternoon, and so it was so close to sundown when we got home that we never stopped on our road, but made a break for the sycamores as tight as we could go, to tell Jake what the delay was, and have him wait till we could go to Brace's and find out how things was there. It was getting pretty dim by the time we turned the corner of the woods, sweating and panting with that long run, and see the sycamores thirty yards ahead of us; and just then we see a couple of men run into the bunch and heard two or three terrible screams for help. "Poor Jake is killed, sure," we says. We was scared through and through, and broke for the tobacker field and hid there, trembling so our clothes would hardly stay on; and just as we skipped in there, a couple of men went tearing by, and into the bunch they went, and in a second out jumps four men and took out up the road as tight as they could go, two chasing two.

We laid down, kind of weak and sick, and listened for more sounds, but didn't hear none for a good while but just our hearts. We was thinking of that awful thing laying yonder in the sycamores, and it seemed like being that close to a ghost, and it give me the cold shudders. The moon come a-swelling up out of the ground, now, powerful big and round and bright, behind a comb of trees, like a face looking through prison bars, and the black shadders and white places begun to creep around, and it was miserable quiet and still and night-breezy and graveyardy and scary. All of a sudden Tom whispers:

"Look! — What's that?"

"Don't!" I says. "Don't take a person by surprise that way. I'm 'most ready to die, anyway, without you doing that."

"Look, I tell you. It's something coming out of the sycamores."

"Don't, Tom!"

"It's terrible tall!"

"Oh, lordy-lordy! let's — "

"Keep still — it's a-coming this way."

He was so excited he could hardly get breath enough to whisper. I had to look. I couldn't help it. So now we was both on our knees with our chins on a fence rail and gazing — yes, and gasping too. It was coming down the road — coming in the shadder of the trees, and you couldn't see it good; not till it was pretty close to us; then it stepped into a bright splotch of moonlight and we sunk right down in our tracks — it was Jake Dunlap's ghost! That was what we said to ourselves.

We couldn't stir for a minute or two; then it was gone. We talked about it in low voices. Tom says:

"They're mostly dim and smoky, or like they're made out of fog, but this one wasn't."

"No," I says; "I seen the goggles and the whiskers perfectly plain."

"Yes, and the very colors in them loud countrified Sunday clothes — plaid breeches, green and black — "

"Cotton velvet westcot, fire-red and yaller squares — "

"Leather straps to the bottoms of the breeches legs and one of them hanging unbottoned — "

"Yes, and that hat — "

"What a hat for a ghost to wear!"

You see it was the first season anybody wore that kind — a black stiff-brim stove-pipe, very high, and not smooth, with a round top — just like a sugar-loaf.

"Did you notice if its hair was the same, Huck?"

"No — seems to me I did, then again it seems to me I didn't."

"I didn't either; but it had its bag along, I noticed that."

"So did I. How can there be a ghost-bag, Tom?"

"Sho! I wouldn't be as ignorant as that if I was you, Huck Finn. Whatever a ghost has, turns to ghost-stuff. They've got to have their things, like anybody else. You see, yourself, that its clothes was turned to ghost-stuff. Well, then, what's to hender its bag from turning, too? Of course it done it."

That was reasonable. I couldn't find no fault with it. Bill Withers and his brother Jack come along by, talking, and Jack says:

"What do you reckon he was toting?"

"I dunno; but it was pretty heavy."

"Yes, all he could lug. Nigger stealing corn from old Parson Silas, I judged."

"So did I. And so I allowed I wouldn't let on to see him."

"That's me, too."

Then they both laughed, and went on out of hearing. It showed how un-popular old Uncle Silas had got to be now. They wouldn't 'a' let a nigger steal anybody else's corn and never done anything to him.

We heard some more voices mumbling along towards us and getting louder, and sometimes a cackle of a laugh. It was Lem Beebe and Jim Lane. Jim Lane says:

"Who? — Jubiter Dunlap?"

"Yes."

"Oh, I don't know. I reckon so. I seen him spading up some ground along about an hour ago, just before sundown — him and the parson. Said he guessed he wouldn't go to-night, but we could have his dog if we wanted him."

"Too tired, I reckon."

"Yes — works so hard!"

"Oh, you bet!"

They cackled at that, and went on by. Tom said we better jump out and tag along after them, because they was going our way and it wouldn't be comfortable to run across the ghost all by ourselves. So we done it, and got home all right.

That night was the second of September — a Saturday. I sha'n't ever forget it. You'll see why, pretty soon.

CHAPTER **VI** – Plans to Secure the Diamonds

W E TRAMPED ALONG BEHIND Jim and Lem till we come to the back stile where old Jim's cabin was that he was captivated in, the time we set him free, and here come the dogs piling around us to say howdy, and there was the lights of the house, too; so we warn't afeard any more, and was going to climb over, but Tom says:

"Hold on; set down here a minute. By George!"

"What's the matter?" says I.

"Matter enough!" he says. "Wasn't you expecting we would be the first to tell the family who it is that's been killed yonder in the sycamores, and all about them rapscallions that done it, and about the di'monds they've smouched off of the corpse, and paint it up fine, and have the glory of being the ones that knows a lot more about it than anybody else?"

"Why, of course. It wouldn't be you, Tom Sawyer, if you was to let such a chance go by. I reckon it ain't going to suffer none for lack of paint," I says, "when you start in to scollop the facts."

"Well, now," he says, perfectly ca'm, "what would you say if I was to tell you I ain't going to start in at all?"

I was astonished to hear him talk so. I says:

"I'd say it's a lie. You ain't in earnest, Tom Sawyer?"

"You'll soon see. Was the ghost barefooted?"

"No, it wasn't. What of it?"

"You wait — I'll show you what. Did it have its boots on?"

"Yes. I seen them plain."

"Swear it?"

"Yes, I swear it."

"So do I. Now do you know what that means?"

"No. What does it mean?"

"Means that them thieves DIDN'T GET THE DI'MONDS."

"Jimminy! What makes you think that?"

"I don't only think it, I know it. Didn't the breeches and goggles and whiskers and hand-bag and every blessed thing turn to ghost-stuff? Everything it had on turned, didn't it? It shows that the reason its boots turned too was because it still had them on after it started to go ha'nting around, and if that ain't proof that them blatherskites didn't get the boots, I'd like to know what you'd CALL proof."

Think of that now. I never see such a head as that boy had. Why, I had eyes and I could see things, but they never meant nothing to me. But Tom Sawyer was different. When Tom Sawyer seen a thing it just got up on its hind legs and TALKED to him — told him everything it knowed. I never see such a head.

"Tom Sawyer," I says, "I'll say it again as I've said it a many a time before: I ain't fitten to black your boots. But that's all right — that's neither here nor there. God Almighty made us all, and some He gives eyes that's blind, and some He gives eyes that can see, and I reckon it ain't none of our lookout what He done it for; it's all right, or He'd 'a' fixed it some other way. Go on — I see plenty plain enough, now, that them thieves didn't get way with the di'monds. Why didn't they, do you reckon?"

"Because they got chased away by them other two men before they could pull the boots off of the corpse."

"That's so! I see it now. But looky here, Tom, why ain't we to go and tell about it?"

"Oh, shucks, Huck Finn, can't you see? Look at it. What's a-going to happen? There's going to be an inquest in the morning. Them two men will tell how they heard the yells and rushed there just in time to not save the stranger. Then the jury'll twaddle and twaddle and twaddle, and finally they'll fetch in a verdict that he got shot or stuck or busted over the head with something, and come to his death by the inspiration of God. And after they've buried him they'll auction off his things for to pay the expenses, and then's OUR chance."

"How, Tom?"

"Buy the boots for two dollars!"

Well, it 'most took my breath.

"My land! Why, Tom, WE'LL get the di'monds!"

"You bet. Some day there'll be a big reward offered for them — a thousand dollars, sure. That's our money! Now we'll trot in and see the folks. And mind you we don't know anything about any murder, or any di'-monds, or any thieves — don't you forget that."

I had to sigh a little over the way he had got it fixed. I'd 'a' SOLD them di'monds — yes, sir — for twelve thousand dollars; but I didn't say anything. It wouldn't done any good. I says:

"But what are we going to tell your aunt Sally has made us so long getting down here from the village, Tom?"

"Oh, I'll leave that to you," he says. "I reckon you can explain it somehow."

He was always just that strict and delicate. He never would tell a lie himself.

We struck across the big yard, noticing this, that, and t'other thing that was so familiar, and we so glad to see it again, and when we got to the roofed big passageway betwixt the double log house and the kitchen part, there was everything hanging on the wall just as it used to was, even to Uncle Silas's old faded green baize working-gown with the hood to it, and raggedy white patch between the shoulders that always looked like somebody had hit him with a snowball; and then we lifted the latch and walked in. Aunt Sally she was just a-ripping and a-tearing around, and the children was huddled in one corner, and the old man he was huddled in the other and praying for help in time of need. She jumped for us with joy and tears running down her face and give us a whacking box on the ear, and then hugged us and kissed us and boxed us again, and just couldn't seem to get enough of it, she was so glad to see us; and she says:

"Where HAVE you been a-loafing to, you good-for-nothing trash! I've been that worried about you I didn't know what to do. Your traps has been here ever so long, and I've had supper cooked fresh about four times so as to have it hot and good when you come, till at last my patience is just plumb wore out, and I declare I — I — why I could skin you alive! You must be starving, poor things! — Set down, set down, everybody; don't lose no more time."

It was good to be there again behind all that noble corn-pone and spareribs, and everything that you could ever want in this world. Old Uncle Silas he peeled off one of his bulliest old-time blessings, with as many layers to it as an onion, and whilst the angels was hauling in the slack of it I was trying to study up what to say about what kept us so long. When our plates was all loadened and we'd got a-going, she asked me, and I says:

"Well, you see, — er — Mizzes — "

"Huck Finn! Since when am I Mizzes to you? Have I ever been stingy of cuffs or kisses for you since the day you stood in this room and I took you for Tom Sawyer and blessed God for sending you to me, though you told me four thousand lies and I believed every one of them like a simpleton? Call me Aunt Sally — like you always done."

So I done it. And I says:

"Well, me and Tom allowed we would come along afoot and take a smell of the woods, and we run across Lem Beebe and Jim Lane, and they asked us to go with them blackberrying to-night, and said they could borrow Jubiter Dunlap's dog, because he had told them just that minute — "

"Where did they see him?" says the old man; and when I looked up to see how HE come to take an intrust in a little thing like that, his eyes was just burning into me, he was that eager. It surprised me so it kind of throwed me off, but I pulled myself together again and says:

"It was when he was spading up some ground along with you, towards sundown or along there."

He only said, "Um," in a kind of a disappointed way, and didn't take no more intrust. So I went on. I says:

"Well, then, as I was a-saying — "

"That'll do, you needn't go no furder." It was Aunt Sally. She was boring right into me with her eyes, and very indignant. "Huck Finn," she says, "how'd them men come to talk about going a-black-berrying in September — in THIS region?"

I see I had slipped up, and I couldn't say a word. She waited, still a-gazing at me, then she says:

"And how'd they come to strike that idiot idea of going a-blackberrying in the night?"

"Well, m'm, they — er — they told us they had a lantern, and — "

"Oh, SHET up — do! Looky here; what was they going to do with a dog? — hunt blackberries with it?"

"I think, m'm, they — "

"Now, Tom Sawyer, what kind of a lie are you fixing YOUR mouth to contribit to this mess of rubbage? Speak out — and I warn you before you begin, that I don't believe a word of it. You and Huck's been up to something you no business to — I know it perfectly well; I know you, BOTH of you. Now you explain that dog, and them blackberries, and the lantern, and the rest of that rot — and mind you talk as straight as a string — do you hear?"

Tom he looked considerable hurt, and says, very dignified:

"It is a pity if Huck is to be talked to that way, just for making a little bit of a mistake that anybody could make."

"What mistake has he made?"

"Why, only the mistake of saying blackberries when of course he meant strawberries."

"Tom Sawyer, I lay if you aggravate me a little more, I'll — "

"Aunt Sally, without knowing it — and of course without intending it — you are in the wrong. If you'd 'a' studied natural history the way you ought, you would know that all over the world except just here in Arkansaw they ALWAYS hunt strawberries with a dog — and a lantern — "

But she busted in on him there and just piled into him and snowed him under. She was so mad she couldn't get the words out fast enough, and she gushed them out in one everlasting freshet. That was what Tom Sawyer was after. He allowed to work her up and get her started and then leave her alone and let her burn herself out. Then she would be so aggravated with that subject that she wouldn't say another word about it, nor let anybody else. Well, it happened just so. When she was tuckered out and had to hold up, he says, quite ca'm:

"And yet, all the same, Aunt Sally — "

"Shet up!" she says, "I don't want to hear another word out of you."

So we was perfectly safe, then, and didn't have no more trouble about that delay. Tom done it elegant.

CHAPTER VII – A Night's Vigil

BENNY SHE WAS LOOKING PRETTY SOBER, and she sighed some, now and then; but pretty soon she got to asking about Mary, and Sid, and Tom's aunt Polly, and then Aunt Sally's clouds cleared off and she got in a good humor and joined in on the questions and was her lovingest best self, and so the rest of the supper went along gay and pleasant. But the old man he didn't take any hand hardly, and was absent-minded and restless, and done a considerable amount of sighing; and it was kind of heart-breaking to see him so sad and troubled and worried.

By and by, a spell after supper, come a nigger and knocked on the door and put his head in with his old straw hat in his hand bowing and scraping, and said his Marse Brace was out at the stile and wanted his brother, and was getting tired waiting supper for him, and would Marse Silas please tell him where he was? I never see Uncle Silas speak up so sharp and fractious before. He says:

"Am I his brother's keeper?" And then he kind of wilted together, and looked like he wished he hadn't spoken so, and then he says, very gentle: "But you needn't say that, Billy; I was took sudden and irritable, and I ain't very well these days, and not hardly responsible. Tell him he ain't here."

And when the nigger was gone he got up and walked the floor, backwards and forwards, mumbling and muttering to himself and plowing his hands through his hair. It was real pitiful to see him. Aunt Sally she whispered to us and told us not to take notice of him, it embarrassed him. She said he was always thinking and thinking, since these troubles come on, and she allowed he didn't more'n about half know what he was about when the thinking spells was on him; and she said he walked in his sleep considerable more now than he used to, and sometimes wandered around over the house and even outdoors in his sleep, and if we catched him at it we must let him alone and not disturb him. She said she reckoned it didn't do him no harm, and may be it done him good. She said Benny was the only one that was much help to him these days. Said Benny appeared to know just when to try to soothe him and when to leave him alone.

So he kept on tramping up and down the floor and muttering, till by and by he begun to look pretty tired; then Benny she went and snuggled up to his side and put one hand in his and one arm around his waist and walked with him; and he smiled down on her, and reached down and kissed her; and so, little by little the trouble went out of his face and she persuaded him off to his room. They had very petting ways together, and it was uncommon pretty to see.

Aunt Sally she was busy getting the children ready for bed; so by and by it got dull and tedious, and me and Tom took a turn in the moonlight, and fetched up in the watermelon-patch and et one, and had a good deal of talk. And Tom said he'd bet the quarreling was all Jubiter's fault, and he was going to be on hand the first time he got a chance, and see; and if it was so, he was going to do his level best to get Uncle Silas to turn him off.

And so we talked and smoked and stuffed watermelons much as two hours, and then it was pretty late, and when we got back the house was quiet and dark, and everybody gone to bed.

Tom he always seen everything, and now he see that the old green baize work-gown was gone, and said it wasn't gone when he went out; so he allowed it was curious, and then we went up to bed.

We could hear Benny stirring around in her room, which was next to ourn, and judged she was worried a good deal about her father and couldn't sleep. We found we couldn't, neither. So we set up a long time, and smoked and talked in a low voice, and felt pretty dull and down-hearted. We talked the murder and the ghost over and over again, and got so creepy and crawly we couldn't get sleepy nohow and noway.

By and by, when it was away late in the night and all the sounds was late sounds and solemn, Tom nudged me and whispers to me to look, and I done it, and there we see a man poking around in the yard like he didn't know just what he wanted to do, but it was pretty dim and we couldn't see him good. Then he started for the stile, and as he went over it the moon came out strong, and he had a long-handled shovel over his shoulder, and we see the white patch on the old work-gown. So Tom says:

"He's a-walking in his sleep. I wish we was allowed to follow him and see where he's going to. There, he's turned down by the tobacker-field. Out of sight now. It's a dreadful pity he can't rest no better."

We waited a long time, but he didn't come back any more, or if he did he come around the other way; so at last we was tuckered out and went to sleep and had nightmares, a million of them. But before dawn we was awake again, because meantime a storm had come up and been raging, and the thunder and lightning was awful, and the wind was a-thrashing the trees around, and the rain was driving down in slanting sheets, and the gullies was running rivers. Tom says:

"Looky here, Huck, I'll tell you one thing that's mighty curious. Up to the time we went out last night the family hadn't heard about Jake Dunlap being murdered. Now the men that chased Hal Clayton and Bud Dixon away would spread the thing around in a half an hour, and every neighbor that heard it would shin out and fly around from one farm to t'other and try to be the first to tell the news. Land, they don't have such a big thing as that to tell twice in thirty year! Huck, it's mighty strange; I don't understand it."

So then he was in a fidget for the rain to let up, so we could turn out and run across some of the people and see if they would say anything about it to us. And he said if they did we must be horribly surprised and shocked.

We was out and gone the minute the rain stopped. It was just broad day then. We loafed along up the road, and now and then met a person and stopped and said howdy, and told them when we come, and how we left the folks at home, and how long we was going to stay, and all that, but none of them said a word about that thing; which was just astonishing, and no mistake. Tom said he believed if we went to the sycamores we would find that body laying there solitary and alone, and not a soul around. Said he believed the men chased the thieves so far into the woods that the thieves prob'ly seen a good chance and turned on them at last, and maybe they all killed each other, and so there wasn't anybody left to tell.

First we knowed, gabbling along that away, we was right at the sycamores. The cold chills trickled down my back and I wouldn't budge another step, for all Tom's persuading. But he couldn't hold in; he'd GOT to see if the boots was safe on that body yet. So he crope in — and the next minute out he come again with his eyes bulging he was so excited, and says:

"Huck, it's gone!"

I WAS astonished! I says:

"Tom, you don't mean it."

"It's gone, sure. There ain't a sign of it. The ground is trampled some, but if there was any blood it's all washed away by the storm, for it's all puddles and slush in there."

At last I give in, and went and took a look myself; and it was just as Tom said — there wasn't a sign of a corpse.

"Dern it," I says, "the di'monds is gone. Don't you reckon the thieves slunk back and lugged him off, Tom?"

"Looks like it. It just does. Now where'd they hide him, do you reckon?"

"I don't know," I says, disgusted, "and what's more I don't care. They've got the boots, and that's all I cared about. He'll lay around these woods a long time before I hunt him up."

Tom didn't feel no more intrust in him neither, only curiosity to know what come of him; but he said we'd lay low and keep dark and it wouldn't be long till the dogs or somebody rousted him out.

We went back home to breakfast ever so bothered and put out and disappointed and swindled. I warn't ever so down on a corpse before.

CHAPTER **VIII** – Talking with the Ghost

I T WARN'T VERY CHEERFUL at breakfast. Aunt Sally she looked old and tired and let the children snarl and fuss at one another and didn't seem to notice it was going on, which wasn't her usual style; me and Tom had a plenty to think about without talking; Benny she looked like she hadn't had much sleep, and whenever she'd lift her head a little and steal a look towards her father you could see there was tears in her eyes; and as for the old man, his things stayed on his plate and got cold without him knowing they was there, I reckon, for he was thinking and thinking all the time, and never said a word and never et a bite.

By and by when it was stillest, that nigger's head was poked in at the door again, and he said his Marse Brace was getting powerful uneasy about Marse Jubiter, which hadn't come home yet, and would Marse Silas please — He was looking at Uncle Silas, and he stopped there, like the rest of his words was froze; for Uncle Silas he rose up shaky and steadied himself leaning his fingers on the table, and he was panting, and his eyes was set on the nigger, and he kept swallowing, and put his other hand up to his throat a couple of times, and at last he got his words started, and says:

"Does he — does he — think — WHAT does he think! Tell him — tell him — " Then he sunk down in his chair limp and weak, and says, so as you could hardly hear him: "Go away — go away!"

The nigger looked scared and cleared out, and we all felt — well, I don't know how we felt, but it was awful, with the old man panting there, and his

eyes set and looking like a person that was dying. None of us could budge; but Benny she slid around soft, with her tears running down, and stood by his side, and nestled his old gray head up against her and begun to stroke it and pet it with her hands, and nodded to us to go away, and we done it, going out very quiet, like the dead was there.

Me and Tom struck out for the woods mighty solemn, and saying how different it was now to what it was last summer when we was here and everything was so peaceful and happy and everybody thought so much of Uncle Silas, and he was so cheerful and simple-hearted and pudd'n-headed and good — and now look at him. If he hadn't lost his mind he wasn't much short of it. That was what we allowed.

It was a most lovely day now, and bright and sunshiny; and the further and further we went over the hills towards the prairie the lovelier and lovelier the trees and flowers got to be and the more it seemed strange and somehow wrong that there had to be trouble in such a world as this. And then all of a sudden I catched my breath and grabbed Tom's arm, and all my livers and lungs and things fell down into my legs.

"There it is!" I says. We jumped back behind a bush shivering, and Tom says:

"'Sh! — don't make a noise."

It was setting on a log right in the edge of a little prairie, thinking. I tried to get Tom to come away, but he wouldn't, and I dasn't budge by myself. He said we mightn't ever get another chance to see one, and he was going to look his fill at this one if he died for it. So I looked too, though it give me the fan-tods to do it. Tom he HAD to talk, but he talked low. He says:

"Poor Jakey, it's got all its things on, just as he said he would. NOW you see what we wasn't certain about — its hair. It's not long now the way it was: it's got it cropped close to its head, the way he said he would. Huck, I never see anything look any more naturaler than what it does."

"Nor I neither," I says; "I'd recognize it anywheres."

"So would I. It looks perfectly solid and genuwyne, just the way it done before it died."

So we kept a-gazing. Pretty soon Tom says:

"Huck, there's something mighty curious about this one, don't you know? It oughtn't to be going around in the daytime."

"That's so, Tom — I never heard the like of it before."

"No, sir, they don't ever come out only at night — and then not till after twelve. There's something wrong about this one, now you mark my words. I don't believe it's got any right to be around in the daytime. But don't it look natural! Jake was going to play deef and dumb here, so the neighbors wouldn't know his voice. Do you reckon it would do that if we was to holler at it?"

"Lordy, Tom, don't talk so! If you was to holler at it I'd die in my tracks."

"Don't you worry, I ain't going to holler at it. Look, Huck, it's a-scratching its head — don't you see?"

"Well, what of it?"

"Why, this. What's the sense of it scratching its head? There ain't anything there to itch; its head is made out of fog or something like that, and can't itch. A fog can't itch; any fool knows that."

"Well, then, if it don't itch and can't itch, what in the nation is it scratching it for? Ain't it just habit, don't you reckon?"

"No, sir, I don't. I ain't a bit satisfied about the way this one acts. I've a blame good notion it's a bogus one — I have, as sure as I'm a-sitting here. Because, if it — Huck!"

"Well, what's the matter now?"

"YOU CAN'T SEE THE BUSHES THROUGH IT!"

"Why, Tom, it's so, sure! It's as solid as a cow. I sort of begin to think — "

"Huck, it's biting off a chaw of tobacker! By George, THEY don't chaw — they hain't got anything to chaw WITH. Huck!"

"I'm a-listening."

"It ain't a ghost at all. It's Jake Dunlap his own self!"

"Oh your granny!" I says.

"Huck Finn, did we find any corpse in the sycamores?"

"No."

"Or any sign of one?"

"No."

"Mighty good reason. Hadn't ever been any corpse there."

"Why, Tom, you know we heard — "

"Yes, we did — heard a howl or two. Does that prove anybody was killed? Course it don't. And we seen four men run, then this one come walking out and we took it for a ghost. No more ghost than you are. It was Jake Dunlap his own self, and it's Jake Dunlap now. He's been and got his hair cropped, the way he said he would, and he's playing himself for a stranger, just the same as he said he would. Ghost? Hum! — he's as sound as a nut."

Then I see it all, and how we had took too much for granted. I was powerful glad he didn't get killed, and so was Tom, and we wondered which he would like the best — for us to never let on to know him, or how? Tom reckoned the best way would be to go and ask him. So he started; but I kept a little behind, because I didn't know but it might be a ghost, after all. When Tom got to where he was, he says:

"Me and Huck's mighty glad to see you again, and you needn't be afeared we'll tell. And if you think it'll be safer for you if we don't let on to know you when we run across you, say the word and you'll see you can depend on us, and would ruther cut our hands off than get you into the least little bit of danger."

First off he looked surprised to see us, and not very glad, either; but as Tom went on he looked pleasanter, and when he was done he smiled, and nodded his head several times, and made signs with his hands, and says:

"Goo-goo — goo-goo," the way deef and dummies does.

Just then we see some of Steve Nickerson's people coming that lived t'other side of the prairie, so Tom says:

"You do it elegant; I never see anybody do it better. You're right; play it on us, too; play it on us same as the others; it'll keep you in practice and prevent you making blunders. We'll keep away from you and let on we don't know you, but any time we can be any help, you just let us know."

Then we loafed along past the Nickersons, and of course they asked if that was the new stranger yonder, and where'd he come from, and what was his name, and which communion was he, Babtis' or Methodis', and which politics, Whig or Democrat, and how long is he staying, and all them other questions that humans always asks when a stranger comes, and animals does, too. But Tom said he warn't able to make anything out of deef and dumb signs, and the same with goo-gooing. Then we watched them go and bullyrag Jake; because we was pretty uneasy for him. Tom said it would take him days to get so he wouldn't forget he was a deef and dummy sometimes, and speak out before he thought. When we had watched long enough to see that Jake was getting along all right and working his signs very good, we loafed along again, allowing to strike the schoolhouse about recess time, which was a three-mile tramp.

I was so disappointed not to hear Jake tell about the row in the sycamores, and how near he come to getting killed, that I couldn't seem to get over it, and Tom he felt the same, but said if we was in Jake's fix we would want to go careful and keep still and not take any chances.

The boys and girls was all glad to see us again, and we had a real good time all through recess. Coming to school the Henderson boys had come across the new deef and dummy and told the rest; so all the scholars was chuck full of him and couldn't talk about anything else, and was in a sweat to get a sight of him because they hadn't ever seen a deef and dummy in their lives, and it made a powerful excitement.

Tom said it was tough to have to keep mum now; said we would be heroes if we could come out and tell all we knowed; but after all, it was still more heroic to keep mum, there warn't two boys in a million could do it. That was Tom Sawyer's idea about it, and I reckoned there warn't anybody could better it.

CHAPTER IX – Finding of Jubiter Dunlap

IN THE NEXT TWO OR THREE DAYS Dummy he got to be powerful popular. He went associating around with the neighbors, and they made much of him, and was proud to have such a rattling curiosity among them. They had him to breakfast, they had him to dinner, they had him to supper; they kept him loaded up with hog and hominy, and warn't ever tired staring at him and wondering over him, and wishing they knowed more about him, he was so uncommon and romantic. His signs warn't no good; people couldn't understand them and he prob'ly couldn't himself, but he done a sight of goo-gooing, and so everybody was satisfied, and admired to hear him go it. He toted a piece of slate around, and a pencil; and people wrote questions on it and he wrote answers; but there warn't anybody could read his writing but Brace Dunlap. Brace said he couldn't read it very good, but he could manage to dig out the meaning most of the time. He said Dummy said he belonged away off somers and used to be well off, but got busted by swindlers which he had trusted, and was poor now, and hadn't any way to make a living.

Everybody praised Brace Dunlap for being so good to that stranger. He let him have a little log-cabin all to himself, and had his niggers take care of it, and fetch him all the vittles he wanted.

Dummy was at our house some, because old Uncle Silas was so afflicted himself, these days, that anybody else that was afflicted was a comfort to him. Me and Tom didn't let on that we had knowed him before, and he didn't let on that he had knowed us before. The family talked their troubles out before him the same as if he wasn't there, but we reckoned it wasn't any harm for him to hear what they said. Generly he didn't seem to notice, but sometimes he did.

Well, two or three days went along, and everybody got to getting uneasy about Jubiter Dunlap. Everybody was asking everybody if they had any idea what had become of him. No, they hadn't, they said: and they shook their heads and said there was something powerful strange about it. Another and another day went by; then there was a report got around that praps he was murdered. You bet it made a big stir! Everybody's tongue was clacking away after that. Saturday two or three gangs turned out and hunted the woods to see if they could run across his remainders. Me and Tom helped, and it was noble good times and exciting. Tom he was so brimful of it he couldn't eat nor rest. He said if we could find that corpse we would be celebrated, and more talked about than if we got drownded.

The others got tired and give it up; but not Tom Sawyer — that warn't his style. Saturday night he didn't sleep any, hardly, trying to think up a plan; and towards daylight in the morning he struck it. He snaked me out of bed and was all excited, and says:

"Quick, Huck, snatch on your clothes — I've got it! Bloodhound!"

In two minutes we was tearing up the river road in the dark towards the village. Old Jeff Hooker had a bloodhound, and Tom was going to borrow him. I says:

"The trail's too old, Tom — and besides, it's rained, you know."

"It don't make any difference, Huck. If the body's hid in the woods anywhere around the hound will find it. If he's been murdered and buried, they wouldn't bury him deep, it ain't likely, and if the dog goes over the spot he'll scent him, sure. Huck, we're going to be celebrated, sure as you're born!"

He was just a-blazing; and whenever he got afire he was most likely to get

afire all over. That was the way this time. In two minutes he had got it all ci-
phered out, and wasn't only just going to find the corpse — no, he was
going to get on the track of that murderer and hunt HIM down, too; and not
only that, but he was going to stick to him till — "Well," I says, "you better
find the corpse first; I reckon that's a-plenty for to-day. For all we know,
there AIN'T any corpse and nobody hain't been murdered. That cuss could
'a' gone off somers and not been killed at all."

That graveled him, and he says:

"Huck Finn, I never see such a person as you to want to spoil everything.
As long as YOU can't see anything hopeful in a thing, you won't let anybody
else. What good can it do you to throw cold water on that corpse and get up
that selfish theory that there ain't been any murder? None in the world. I
don't see how you can act so. I wouldn't treat you like that, and you know
it. Here we've got a noble good opportunity to make a ruputation, and — "

"Oh, go ahead," I says. "I'm sorry, and I take it all back. I didn't mean
nothing. Fix it any way you want it. HE ain't any consequence to me. If he's
killed, I'm as glad of it as you are; and if he — "

"I never said anything about being glad; I only — "

"Well, then, I'm as SORRY as you are. Any way you druther have it, that
is the way I druther have it. He — "

"There ain't any druthers ABOUT it, Huck Finn; nobody said anything
about druthers. And as for — "

He forgot he was talking, and went tramping along, studying. He begun
to get excited again, and pretty soon he says:

"Huck, it'll be the bulliest thing that ever happened if we find the body
after everybody else has quit looking, and then go ahead and hunt up the
murderer. It won't only be an honor to us, but it'll be an honor to Uncle
Silas because it was us that done it. It'll set him up again, you see if it don't."

But Old Jeff Hooker he threwed cold water on the whole business when
we got to his blacksmith shop and told him what we come for.

"You can take the dog," he says, "but you ain't a-going to find any corpse, because there ain't any corpse to find. Everybody's quit looking, and they're right. Soon as they come to think, they knowed there warn't no corpse. And I'll tell you for why. What does a person kill another person for, Tom Sawyer? — answer me that."

"Why, he — er — "

"Answer up! You ain't no fool. What does he kill him FOR?"

"Well, sometimes it's for revenge, and — "

"Wait. One thing at a time. Revenge, says you; and right you are. Now who ever had anything agin that poor trifling no-account? Who do you reckon would want to kill HIM? — that rabbit!"

Tom was stuck. I reckon he hadn't thought of a person having to have a REASON for killing a person before, and now he sees it warn't likely anybody would have that much of a grudge against a lamb like Jubiter Dunlap. The blacksmith says, by and by:

"The revenge idea won't work, you see. Well, then, what's next? Robbery? B'gosh, that must 'a' been it, Tom! Yes, sirree, I reckon we've struck it this time. Some feller wanted his gallus-buckles, and so he — "

But it was so funny he busted out laughing, and just went on laughing and laughing and laughing till he was 'most dead, and Tom looked so put out and cheap that I knowed he was ashamed he had come, and he wished he hadn't. But old Hooker never let up on him. He raked up everything a person ever could want to kill another person about, and any fool could see they didn't any of them fit this case, and he just made no end of fun of the whole business and of the people that had been hunting the body; and he said:

"If they'd had any sense they'd 'a' knowed the lazy cuss slid out because he wanted a loafing spell after all this work. He'll come pottering back in a couple of weeks, and then how'll you fellers feel? But, laws bless you, take the dog, and go and hunt his remainders. Do, Tom."

Then he busted out, and had another of them forty-rod laughs of hisn.

Tom couldn't back down after all this, so he said, "All right, unchain him;" and the blacksmith done it, and we started home and left that old man laughing yet.

It was a lovely dog. There ain't any dog that's got a lovelier disposition than a bloodhound, and this one knowed us and liked us. He capered and raced around ever so friendly, and powerful glad to be free and have a holiday; but Tom was so cut up he couldn't take any intrust in him, and said he wished he'd stopped and thought a minute before he ever started on such a fool errand. He said old Jeff Hooker would tell everybody, and we'd never hear the last of it.

So we loafed along home down the back lanes, feeling pretty glum and not talking. When we was passing the far corner of our tobacker field we heard the dog set up a long howl in there, and we went to the place and he was scratching the ground with all his might, and every now and then canting up his head sideways and fetching another howl.

It was a long square, the shape of a grave; the rain had made it sink down and show the shape. The minute we come and stood there we looked at one another and never said a word. When the dog had dug down only a few inches he grabbed something and pulled it up, and it was an arm and a sleeve. Tom kind of gasped out, and says:

"Come away, Huck — it's found."

I just felt awful. We struck for the road and fetched the first men that come along. They got a spade at the crib and dug out the body, and you never see such an excitement. You couldn't make anything out of the face, but you didn't need to. Everybody said:

"Poor Jubiter; it's his clothes, to the last rag!"

Some rushed off to spread the news and tell the justice of the peace and have an inquest, and me and Tom lit out for the house. Tom was all afire and 'most out of breath when we come tearing in where Uncle Silas and Aunt Sally and Benny was. Tom sung out:

"Me and Huck's found Jubiter Dunlap's corpse all by ourselves with a bloodhound, after everybody else had quit hunting and given it up; and if it hadn't a been for us it never WOULD 'a' been found; and he WAS murdered too — they done it with a club or something like that; and I'm going to start in and find the murderer, next, and I bet I'll do it!"

Aunt Sally and Benny sprung up pale and astonished, but Uncle Silas fell right forward out of his chair on to the floor and groans out:

"Oh, my God, you've found him NOW!"

CHAPTER X – The Arrest of Uncle Silas

THEM AWFUL WORDS FROZE US SOLID. We couldn't move hand or foot for as much as half a minute. Then we kind of come to, and lifted the old man up and got him into his chair, and Benny petted him and kissed him and tried to comfort him, and poor old Aunt Sally she done the same; but, poor things, they was so broke up and scared and knocked out of their right minds that they didn't hardly know what they was about. With Tom it was awful; it 'most petrified him to think maybe he had got his uncle into a thousand times more trouble than ever, and maybe it wouldn't ever happened if he hadn't been so ambitious to get celebrated, and let the corpse alone the way the others done. But pretty soon he sort of come to himself again and says:

"Uncle Silas, don't you say another word like that. It's dangerous, and there ain't a shadder of truth in it."

Aunt Sally and Benny was thankful to hear him say that, and they said the same; but the old man he wagged his head sorrowful and hopeless, and the tears run down his face, and he says;

"No — I done it; poor Jubiter, I done it!"

It was dreadful to hear him say it. Then he went on and told about it, and said it happened the day me and Tom come — along about sundown. He said Jubiter pestered him and aggravated him till he was so mad he just sort of lost his mind and grabbed up a stick and hit him over the head with all his might, and Jubiter dropped in his tracks. Then he was scared and sorry, and got down on his knees and lifted his head up, and begged him to speak and say he wasn't dead; and before long he come to, and when he see who it was holding his head, he jumped like he was 'most scared to death, and cleared the fence and tore into the woods, and was gone. So he hoped he wasn't hurt bad.

"But laws," he says, "it was only just fear that gave him that last little spurt of strength, and of course it soon played out and he laid down in the bush, and there wasn't anybody to help him, and he died."

Then the old man cried and grieved, and said he was a murderer and the mark of Cain was on him, and he had disgraced his family and was going to be found out and hung. But Tom said:

"No, you ain't going to be found out. You DIDN'T kill him. ONE lick wouldn't kill him. Somebody else done it."

"Oh, yes," he says, "I done it — nobody else. Who else had anything against him? Who else COULD have anything against him?"

He looked up kind of like he hoped some of us could mention somebody that could have a grudge against that harmless no-account, but of course it warn't no use — he HAD us; we couldn't say a word. He noticed that, and he saddened down again, and I never see a face so miserable and so pitiful to see. Tom had a sudden idea, and says:

"But hold on! — somebody BURIED him. Now who — "

He shut off sudden. I knowed the reason. It give me the cold shudders when he said them words, because right away I remembered about us seeing Uncle Silas prowling around with a long-handled shovel away in the night that night. And I knowed Benny seen him, too, because she was talking about it one day. The minute Tom shut off he changed the subject and went to begging Uncle Silas to keep mum, and the rest of us done the same, and said he MUST, and said it wasn't his business to tell on himself, and if he kept mum nobody would ever know; but if it was found out and any harm come to him it would break the family's hearts and kill them, and yet never do anybody any good. So at last he promised. We was all of us more comfortable, then, and went to work to cheer up the old man. We told him all he'd got to do was to keep still, and it wouldn't be long till the whole thing would blow over and be forgot. We all said there wouldn't anybody ever suspect Uncle Silas, nor ever dream of such a thing, he being so good and kind, and having such a good character; and Tom says, cordial and hearty, he says:

"Why, just look at it a minute; just consider. Here is Uncle Silas, all these years a preacher — at his own expense; all these years doing good with all his might and every way he can think of — at his own expense, all the time; always been loved by everybody, and respected; always been peaceable and minding his own business, the very last man in this whole deestrict to touch a person, and everybody knows it. Suspect HIM? Why, it ain't any more possible than — "

"By authority of the State of Arkansaw, I arrest you for the murder of Jubiter Dunlap!" shouts the sheriff at the door.

It was awful. Aunt Sally and Benny flung themselves at Uncle Silas, screaming and crying, and hugged him and hung to him, and Aunt Sally said go away, she wouldn't ever give him up, they shouldn't have him, and the niggers they come crowding and crying to the door and — well, I couldn't stand it; it was enough to break a person's heart; so I got out.

They took him up to the little one-horse jail in the village, and we all went along to tell him good-bye; and Tom was feeling elegant, and says to me, "We'll have a most noble good time and heaps of danger some dark night getting him out of there, Huck, and it'll be talked about everywheres and we will be celebrated;" but the old man busted that scheme up the minute he whispered to him about it. He said no, it was his duty to stand whatever the law done to him, and he would stick to the jail plumb through to the end, even if there warn't no door to it. It disappointed Tom and graveled him a good deal, but he had to put up with it.

But he felt responsible and bound to get his uncle Silas free; and he told Aunt Sally, the last thing, not to worry, because he was going to turn in and work night and day and beat this game and fetch Uncle Silas out innocent; and she was very loving to him and thanked him and said she knowed he would do his very best. And she told us to help Benny take care of the house and the children, and then we had a good-bye cry all around and went back to the farm, and left her there to live with the jailer's wife a month till the trial in October.

CHAPTER XI – Tom Sawyer Discovers the Murderers

WELL, THAT WAS A HARD MONTH on us all. Poor Benny, she kept up the best she could, and me and Tom tried to keep things cheerful there at the house, but it kind of went for nothing, as you may say. It was the same up at the jail. We went up every day to see the old people, but it was awful dreary, because the old man warn't sleeping much, and was walking in his sleep considerable and so he got to looking fagged and miserable, and his mind got shaky, and we all got afraid his troubles would break him down and kill him. And whenever we tried to persuade him to feel cheerfuler, he only shook his head and said if we only knowed what it was to carry around a murderer's load in your heart we wouldn't talk that way. Tom and all of us kept telling him it WASN'T murder, but just accidental killing! but it never made any difference — it was murder, and he wouldn't have it any other way. He actu'ly begun to come out plain and square towards trial time and acknowledge that he TRIED to kill the man. Why, that was awful, you know. It made things seem fifty times as dreadful, and there warn't no more comfort for Aunt Sally and Benny. But he promised he wouldn't say a word about his murder when others was around, and we was glad of that.

Tom Sawyer racked the head off of himself all that month trying to plan some way out for Uncle Silas, and many's the night he kept me up 'most all night with this kind of tiresome work, but he couldn't seem to get on the right track no way. As for me, I reckoned a body might as well give it up, it all looked

so blue and I was so downhearted; but he wouldn't. He stuck to the business right along, and went on planning and thinking and ransacking his head.

So at last the trial come on, towards the middle of October, and we was all in the court. The place was jammed, of course. Poor old Uncle Silas, he looked more like a dead person than a live one, his eyes was so hollow and he looked so thin and so mournful. Benny she set on one side of him and Aunt Sally on the other, and they had veils on, and was full of trouble. But Tom he set by our lawyer, and had his finger in everywheres, of course. The lawyer let him, and the judge let him. He 'most took the business out of the lawyer's hands sometimes; which was well enough, because that was only a mud-turtle of a back-settlement lawyer and didn't know enough to come in when it rains, as the saying is.

They swore in the jury, and then the lawyer for the prostitution got up and begun. He made a terrible speech against the old man, that made him moan and groan, and made Benny and Aunt Sally cry. The way HE told about the murder kind of knocked us all stupid it was so different from the old man's tale. He said he was going to prove that Uncle Silas was SEEN to kill Jubiter Dunlap by two good witnesses, and done it deliberate, and SAID he was going to kill him the very minute he hit him with the club; and they seen him hide Jubiter in the bushes, and they seen that Jubiter was stone-dead. And said Uncle Silas come later and lugged Jubiter down into the tobacker field, and two men seen him do it. And said Uncle Silas turned out, away in the night, and buried Jubiter, and a man seen him at it.

I says to myself, poor old Uncle Silas has been lying about it because he reckoned nobody seen him and he couldn't bear to break Aunt Sally's heart and Benny's; and right he was: as for me, I would 'a' lied the same way, and so would anybody that had any feeling, to save them such misery and sorrow which THEY warn't no ways responsible for. Well, it made our lawyer look pretty sick; and it knocked Tom silly, too, for a little spell, but then he braced up and let on that he warn't worried — but I knowed he

WAS, all the same. And the people — my, but it made a stir amongst them!

And when that lawyer was done telling the jury what he was going to prove, he set down and begun to work his witnesses.

First, he called a lot of them to show that there was bad blood betwixt Uncle Silas and the diseased; and they told how they had heard Uncle Silas threaten the diseased, at one time and another, and how it got worse and worse and everybody was talking about it, and how diseased got afraid of his life, and told two or three of them he was certain Uncle Silas would up and kill him some time or another.

Tom and our lawyer asked them some questions; but it warn't no use, they stuck to what they said.

Next, they called up Lem Beebe, and he took the stand. It come into my mind, then, how Lem and Jim Lane had come along talking, that time, about borrowing a dog or something from Jubiter Dunlap; and that brought up the blackberries and the lantern; and that brought up Bill and Jack Withers, and how they passed by, talking about a nigger stealing Uncle Silas's corn; and that fetched up our old ghost that come along about the same time and scared us so — and here HE was too, and a privileged character, on accounts of his being deef and dumb and a stranger, and they had fixed him a chair inside the railing, where he could cross his legs and be comfortable, whilst the other people was all in a jam so they couldn't hardly breathe. So it all come back to me just the way it was that day; and it made me mournful to think how pleasant it was up to then, and how miserable ever since.

LEM BEEBE, sworn, said — "I was a-coming along, that day, second of September, and Jim Lane was with me, and it was towards sundown, and we heard loud talk, like quarrelling, and we was very close, only the hazel bushes between (that's along the fence); and we heard a voice say, 'I've told you more'n once I'd kill you,' and knowed it was this prisoner's voice; and then we see a club come up above the bushes and down out of sight again, and heard a smashing thump and then a groan or two: and then we crope soft to where we could see, and there laid Jupiter Dunlap dead, and this prisoner standing over him with the club; and the next he hauled the dead man into a clump of bushes and hid him, and then we stooped low, to be out of sight, and got away."

WELL, IT WAS AWFUL. It kind of froze everybody's blood to hear it, and the house was 'most as still whilst he was telling it as if there warn't nobody in it. And when he was done, you could hear them gasp and sigh, all over the house, and look at one another the same as to say, "Ain't it perfectly terrible — ain't it awful!"

Now happened a thing that astonished me. All the time the first witnesses was proving the bad blood and the threats and all that, Tom Sawyer was alive and laying for them; and the minute they was through, he went for them, and done his level best to catch them in lies and spile their testimony. But now, how different. When Lem first begun to talk, and never said anything about speaking to Jubiter or trying to borrow a dog off of him, he was all alive and laying for Lem, and you could see he was getting ready to cross-question him to death pretty soon, and then I judged him and me would go on the stand by and by and tell what we heard him and Jim Lane say. But the next time I looked at Tom I got the cold shivers. Why, he was in the brownest study you ever see — miles and miles away. He warn't hearing a word Lem Beebe was saying; and when he got through he was still in that brown-study, just the same. Our lawyer joggled him, and then he looked up startled, and says, "Take the witness if you want him. Lemme alone — I want to think."

Well, that beat me. I couldn't understand it. And Benny and her mother — oh, they looked sick, they was so troubled. They shoved their veils to one side and tried to get his eye, but it warn't any use, and I couldn't get his eye either. So the mud-turtle he tackled the witness, but it didn't amount to nothing; and he made a mess of it.

Then they called up Jim Lane, and he told the very same story over again, exact. Tom never listened to this one at all, but set there thinking and thinking, miles and miles away. So the mud-turtle went in alone again and come out just as flat as he done before. The lawyer for the prostitution looked very comfortable, but the judge looked disgusted. You see, Tom was just the same as a regular lawyer, nearly, because it was Arkansaw law for a prisoner to choose anybody he wanted to help his lawyer, and Tom had had Uncle Silas shove him into the case, and now he was botching it and you could see the judge didn't like it much. All that the mud-turtle got out of Lem and Jim was this: he asked them:

"Why didn't you go and tell what you saw?"

"We was afraid we would get mixed up in it ourselves. And we was just starting down the river a-hunting for all the week besides; but as soon as we come back we found out they'd been searching for the body, so then we went and told Brace Dunlap all about it."

"When was that?"

"Saturday night, September 9th."

The judge he spoke up and says:

"Mr. Sheriff, arrest these two witnesses on suspicions of being accessionary after the fact to the murder."

The lawyer for the prostitution jumps up all excited, and says:

"Your honor! I protest against this extraordi — "

"Set down!" says the judge, pulling his bowie and laying it on his pulpit. "I beg you to respect the Court."

So he done it. Then he called Bill Withers.

BILL WITHERS, sworn, said: "I was coming along about sundown, Saturday, September 2nd, by the prisoner's field, and my brother Jack was with me and we seen a man toting off something heavy on his back and allowed it was a nigger stealing corn; we couldn't see distinct; next we made out that it was one man carrying another; and the way it hung, so kind of limp, we judged it was somebody that was drunk; and by the man's walk we said it was Parson Silas, and we judged he had found Sam Cooper drunk in the road, which he was always trying to reform him, and was toting him out of danger."

IT MADE THE PEOPLE SHIVER to think of poor old Uncle Silas toting off the diseased down to the place in his tobacker field where the dog dug up the body, but there warn't much sympathy around amongst the faces, and I heard one cuss say "'Tis the coldest blooded work I ever struck, lugging a murdered man around like that, and going to bury him like a animal, and him a preacher at that."

Tom he went on thinking, and never took no notice; so our lawyer took the witness and done the best he could, and it was plenty poor enough.

Then Jack Withers he come on the stand and told the same tale, just like Bill done.

And after him comes Brace Dunlap, and he was looking very mournful, and most crying; and there was a rustle and a stir all around, and everybody got ready to listen, and lots of the women folks said, "Poor cretur, poor cretur," and you could see a many of them wiping their eyes.

BRACE DUNLAP, sworn, said: "I was in considerable trouble a long time about my poor brother, but I reckoned things warn't near so bad as he made out, and I couldn't make myself believe anybody would have the heart to hurt a poor harmless cretur like that" — [by jings, I was sure I seen Tom give a kind of a faint little start, and then look disappointed again] — "and you know I COULDN'T think a preacher would hurt him — it warn't natural to think such an onlikely thing — so I never paid much attention, and now I sha'n't ever, ever forgive myself; for if I had a done different, my poor brother would be with me this day, and not laying yonder murdered, and him so harmless."

He kind of broke down there and choked up, and waited to get his voice;

and people all around said the most pitiful things, and women cried; and it was very still in there, and solemn, and old Uncle Silas, poor thing, he give a groan right out so everybody heard him. Then Brace he went on, "Saturday, September 2nd, he didn't come home to supper. By-and-by I got a little uneasy, and one of my niggers went over to this prisoner's place, but come back and said he warn't there. So I got uneasier and uneasier, and couldn't rest. I went to bed, but I couldn't sleep; and turned out, away late in the night, and went wandering over to this prisoner's place and all around about there a good while, hoping I would run across my poor brother, and never knowing he was out of his troubles and gone to a better shore — " So he broke down and choked up again, and most all the women was crying now. Pretty soon he got another start and says: "But it warn't no use; so at last I went home and tried to get some sleep, but couldn't. Well, in a day or two everybody was uneasy, and they got to talking about this prisoner's threats, and took to the idea, which I didn't take no stock in, that my brother was murdered so they hunted around and tried to find his body, but couldn't and give it up. And so I reckoned he was gone off somers to have a little peace, and would come back to us when his troubles was kind of healed. But late Saturday night, the 9th, Lem Beebe and Jim Lane come to my house and told me all — told me the whole awful 'sassination, and my heart was broke. And THEN I remembered something that hadn't took no hold of me at the time, because reports said this prisoner had took to walking in his sleep and doing all kind of things of no consequence, not knowing what he was about. I will tell you what that thing was that come back into my memory. Away late that awful Saturday night when I was wandering around about this prisoner's place, grieving and troubled, I was down by the corner of the tobacker-field and I heard a sound like digging in a gritty soil; and I crope nearer and peeped through the vines that hung on the rail fence and seen this prisoner SHOVELING — shoveling with a long-handled shovel — heaving earth into a big hole that was most filled up; his back was to me, but it was bright moonlight and I knowed him by his old green baize work-gown with a splattery white patch in the middle of the back like somebody had hit him with a snowball. HE WAS BURYING THE MAN HE'D MURDERED!"

AND HE SLUMPED DOWN in his chair crying and sobbing, and 'most everybody in the house busted out wailing, and crying, and saying, "Oh, it's awful — awful — horrible!" and there was a most tremendous excitement, and you couldn't hear yourself think; and right in the midst of it up jumps old Uncle Silas, white as a sheet, and sings out:

"IT'S TRUE, EVERY WORD — I MURDERED HIM IN COLD BLOOD!"

By Jackson, it petrified them! People rose up wild all over the house, straining and staring for a better look at him, and the judge was hammering with his mallet and the sheriff yelling "Order — order in the court — order!"

And all the while the old man stood there a-quaking and his eyes a-burning, and not looking at his wife and daughter, which was clinging to him and begging him to keep still, but pawing them off with his hands and saying he WOULD clear his black soul from crime, he WOULD heave off this load that was more than he could bear, and he WOULDN'T bear it another hour! And then he raged right along with his awful tale, everybody a-staring and gasping, judge, jury, lawyers, and everybody, and Benny and Aunt Sally crying their hearts out. And by George, Tom Sawyer never looked at him once! Never once — just set there gazing with all his eyes at something else, I couldn't tell what. And so the old man raged right along, pouring his words out like a stream of fire:

"I killed him! I am guilty! But I never had the notion in my life to hurt him or harm him, spite of all them lies about my threatening him, till the very minute I raised the club — then my heart went cold! — Then the pity all went out of it, and I struck to kill! In that one moment all my wrongs come into my mind; all the insults that that man and the scoundrel his brother, there, had put upon me, and how they laid in together to ruin me with the people, and take away my good name, and DRIVE me to some deed that would destroy me and my family that hadn't ever done THEM no harm, so help me God! And they done it in a mean revenge — for why? Because my innocent pure girl here at my side wouldn't marry that rich, insolent, ignorant coward, Brace Dunlap, who's been sniveling here over a brother he never cared a brass farthing for — " [I see Tom give a jump and look glad THIS time, to a dead certainty] " — and in that moment I've told you about, I forgot my God and remembered only my heart's bitterness, God forgive me, and I struck to kill. In one second I was miserably sorry — oh, filled with remorse; but I thought of my poor family, and I MUST hide what I'd done for their sakes; and I did hide that corpse in the bushes; and presently I carried it to the tobacker field; and in the deep night I went with my shovel and buried it where — "

Up jumps Tom and shouts:

"NOW, I've got it!" and waves his hand, oh, ever so fine and starchy, towards the old man, and says:

"Set down! A murder WAS done, but you never had no hand in it!"

Well, sir, you could a heard a pin drop. And the old man he sunk down kind of bewildered in his seat and Aunt Sally and Benny didn't know it, because they was so astonished and staring at Tom with their mouths open and not knowing what they was about. And the whole house the same. I never seen people look so helpless and tangled up, and I hain't ever seen eyes bug out and gaze without a blink the way theirn did. Tom says, perfectly ca'm:

"Your honor, may I speak?"

"For God's sake, yes — go on!" says the judge, so astonished and mixed up he didn't know what he was about hardly.

Then Tom he stood there and waited a second or two — that was for to work up an "effect," as he calls it — then he started in just as ca'm as ever, and says:

"For about two weeks now there's been a little bill sticking on the front of this courthouse offering two thousand dollars reward for a couple of big di'monds — stole at St. Louis. Them di'monds is worth twelve thousand dollars. But never mind about that till I get to it. Now about this murder. I will tell you all about it — how it happened — who done it — every DEtail."

You could see everybody nestle now, and begin to listen for all they was worth.

"This man here, Brace Dunlap, that's been sniveling so about his dead brother that YOU know he never cared a straw for, wanted to marry that young girl there, and she wouldn't have him. So he told Uncle Silas he would make him sorry. Uncle Silas knowed how powerful he was, and how little chance he had against such a man, and he was scared and worried, and done everything he could think of to smooth him over and get him to be good to him: he even took his no-account brother Jubiter on the farm and give him wages and stinted his own family to pay them; and Jubiter done everything his brother could contrive to insult Uncle Silas, and fret and worry him, and try to drive Uncle Silas into doing him a hurt, so as to injure Uncle Silas with the people. And it done it. Everybody turned against him and said the meanest kind of things about him, and it gradully broke his heart — yes, and he was so worried and distressed that often he warn't hardly in his right mind.

"Well, on that Saturday that we've had so much trouble about, two of these witnesses here, Lem Beebe and Jim Lane, come along by where Uncle Silas and Jubiter Dunlap was at work — and that much of what they've said is true, the rest is lies. They didn't hear Uncle Silas say he would kill Jubiter; they didn't hear no blow struck; they didn't see no dead man, and they didn't see Uncle Silas hide anything in the bushes. Look at them now — how they set there, wishing they hadn't been so handy with their tongues; anyway, they'll wish it before I get done.

"That same Saturday evening Bill and Jack Withers DID see one man lugging off another one. That much of what they said is true, and the rest is lies. First off they thought it was a nigger stealing Uncle Silas's corn — you notice it makes them look silly, now, to find out somebody overheard them say that. That's because they found out by and by who it was that was doing the lugging, and THEY know best why they swore here that they took it for Uncle Silas by the gait — which it WASN'T, and they knowed it when they swore to that lie.

"A man out in the moonlight DID see a murdered person put under ground in the tobacker field — but it wasn't Uncle Silas that done the burying. He was in his bed at that very time.

"Now, then, before I go on, I want to ask you if you've ever noticed this: that people, when they're thinking deep, or when they're worried, are most always doing something with their hands, and they don't know it, and don't notice what it is their hands are doing, some stroke their chins; some stroke their noses; some stroke up UNDER their chin with their hand; some twirl a chain, some fumble a button, then there's some that draws a figure or a letter with their finger on their cheek, or under their chin or on their under lip. That's MY way. When I'm restless, or worried, or thinking hard, I draw capital V's on my cheek or on my under lip or under my chin, and never anything BUT capital V's — and half the time I don't notice it and don't know I'm doing it."

That was odd. That is just what I do; only I make an O. And I could see people nodding to one another, same as they do when they mean "THAT's so."

"Now, then, I'll go on. That same Saturday — no, it was the night before — there was a steamboat laying at Flagler's Landing, forty miles above here, and it was raining and storming like the nation. And there was a thief aboard, and he had them two big di'monds that's advertised out here on this courthouse door; and he slipped ashore with his hand-bag and struck out into the dark and the storm, and he was a-hoping he could get to this town all right and be safe. But he had two pals aboard the boat, hiding, and he knowed they was going to kill him the first chance they got and take the di'monds; because all three stole them, and then this fellow he got hold of them and skipped.

"Well, he hadn't been gone more'n ten minutes before his pals found it out, and they jumped ashore and lit out after him. Prob'ly they burnt matches and found his tracks. Anyway, they dogged along after him all day Saturday and kept out of his sight; and towards sundown he come to the bunch of sycamores down by Uncle Silas's field, and he went in there to get a disguise out of his hand-bag and put it on before he showed himself here in the town — and mind you he done that just a little after the time that Uncle Silas was hitting Jubiter Dunlap over the head with a club — for he DID hit him.

"But the minute the pals see that thief slide into the bunch of sycamores, they jumped out of the bushes and slid in after him.

"They fell on him and clubbed him to death.

"Yes, for all he screamed and howled so, they never had no mercy on him, but clubbed him to death. And two men that was running along the road heard him yelling that way, and they made a rush into the sycamore bunch — which was where they was bound for, anyway — and when the pals saw them they lit out and the two new men after them a-chasing them as tight as they could go. But only a minute or two — then these two new men slipped back very quiet into the sycamores.

"THEN what did they do? I will tell you what they done. They found where the thief had got his disguise out of his carpet-sack to put on; so one of them strips and puts on that disguise."

Tom waited a little here, for some more "effect" — then he says, very deliberate:

"The man that put on that dead man's disguise was — JUBITER DUNLAP!"

"Great Scott!" everybody shouted, all over the house, and old Uncle Silas he looked perfectly astonished.

"Yes, it was Jubiter Dunlap. Not dead, you see. Then they pulled off the dead man's boots and put Jubiter Dunlap's old ragged shoes on the corpse and put the corpse's boots on Jubiter Dunlap. Then Jubiter Dunlap stayed where he was, and the other man lugged the dead body off in the twilight; and after midnight he went to Uncle Silas's house, and took his old green work-robe off of the peg where it always hangs in the passage betwixt the house and the kitchen and put it on, and stole the long-handled shovel and went off down into the tobacker field and buried the murdered man."

He stopped, and stood half a minute. Then — "And who do you reckon the murdered man WAS? It was — JAKE Dunlap, the long-lost burglar!"

"Great Scott!"

"And the man that buried him was — BRACE Dunlap, his brother!"

"Great Scott!"

"And who do you reckon is this mowing idiot here that's letting on all these weeks to be a deef and dumb stranger? It's — JUBITER Dunlap!"

My land, they all busted out in a howl, and you never see the like of that excitement since the day you was born. And Tom he made a jump for Jubiter and snaked off his goggles and his false whiskers, and there was the murdered man, sure enough, just as alive as anybody! And Aunt Sally and Benny they went to hugging and crying and kissing and smothering old Uncle Silas to that degree he was more muddled and confused and mushed up in his mind than he ever was before, and that is saying considerable. And next, people begun to yell:

"Tom Sawyer! Tom Sawyer! Shut up everybody, and let him go on! Go on, Tom Sawyer!"

Which made him feel uncommon bully, for it was nuts for Tom Sawyer to be a public character that-away, and a hero, as he calls it. So when it was all quiet, he says:

"There ain't much left, only this. When that man there, Brace Dunlap, had most worried the life and sense out of Uncle Silas till at last he plumb lost his mind and hit this other blatherskite, his brother, with a club, I reckon he seen his chance. Jubiter broke for the woods to hide, and I reckon the game was for him to slide out, in the night, and leave the country. Then Brace would make everybody believe Uncle Silas killed him and hid his body somers; and that would ruin Uncle Silas and drive HIM out of the country — hang him, maybe; I dunno. But when they found their dead brother in the sycamores without knowing him, because he was so battered up, they see they had a better thing; disguise BOTH and bury Jake and dig him up presently all dressed up in Jubiter's clothes, and hire Jim Lane and Bill Withers and the others to swear to some handy lies — which they done. And there they set, now, and I told them they would be looking sick before I got done, and that is the way they're looking now.

"Well, me and Huck Finn here, we come down on the boat with the thieves, and the dead one told us all about the di'monds, and said the others would murder him if they got the chance; and we was going to help him all we could. We was bound for the sycamores when we heard them killing him in there; but we was in there in the early morning after the storm and allowed nobody hadn't been killed, after all. And when we see Jubiter Dunlap here spreading around in the very same disguise Jake told us HE was going to wear, we thought it was Jake his own self — and he was goo-gooing deef and dumb, and THAT was according to agreement.

"Well, me and Huck went on hunting for the corpse after the others quit, and we found it. And was proud, too; but Uncle Silas he knocked us crazy by telling us HE killed the man. So we was mighty sorry we found the body, and was bound to save Uncle Silas's neck if we could; and it was going to be tough work, too, because he wouldn't let us break him out of prison the way we done with our old nigger Jim.

"I done everything I could the whole month to think up some way to save Uncle Silas, but I couldn't strike a thing. So when we come into court to-day I come empty, and couldn't see no chance anywheres. But by and by I had a glimpse of something that set me thinking — just a little wee glimpse —

only that, and not enough to make sure; but it set me thinking hard — and WATCHING, when I was only letting on to think; and by and by, sure enough, when Uncle Silas was piling out that stuff about HIM killing Jubiter Dunlap, I catched that glimpse again, and this time I jumped up and shut down the proceedings, because I KNOWED Jubiter Dunlap was a-setting here before me. I knowed him by a thing which I seen him do — and I remembered it. I'd seen him do it when I was here a year ago."

He stopped then, and studied a minute — laying for an "effect" — I knowed it perfectly well. Then he turned off like he was going to leave the platform, and says, kind of lazy and indifferent:

"Well, I believe that is all."

Why, you never heard such a howl! — and it come from the whole house:

"What WAS it you seen him do? Stay where you are, you little devil! You think you are going to work a body up till his mouth's a-watering and stop there? What WAS it he done?"

That was it, you see — he just done it to get an "effect"; you couldn't 'a' pulled him off of that platform with a yoke of oxen.

"Oh, it wasn't anything much," he says. "I seen him looking a little excited when he found Uncle Silas was actually fixing to hang himself for a murder that warn't ever done; and he got more and more nervous and worried, I a-watching him sharp but not seeming to look at him — and all of a sudden his hands begun to work and fidget, and pretty soon his left crept up and HIS FINGER DRAWED A CROSS ON HIS CHEEK, and then I HAD him!"

Well, then they ripped and howled and stomped and clapped their hands till Tom Sawyer was that proud and happy he didn't know what to do with himself.

And then the judge he looked down over his pulpit and says:

"My boy, did you SEE all the various details of this strange conspiracy and tragedy that you've been describing?"

"No, your honor, I didn't see any of them."

"Didn't see any of them! Why, you've told the whole history straight through, just the same as if you'd seen it with your eyes. How did you manage that?"

Tom says, kind of easy and comfortable:

"Oh, just noticing the evidence and piecing this and that together, your honor; just an ordinary little bit of detective work; anybody could 'a' done it."

"Nothing of the kind! Not two in a million could 'a' done it. You are a very remarkable boy."

Then they let go and give Tom another smashing round, and he — well, he wouldn't 'a' sold out for a silver mine. Then the judge says:

"But are you certain you've got this curious history straight?"

"Perfectly, your honor. Here is Brace Dunlap — let him deny his share of it if he wants to take the chance; I'll engage to make him wish he hadn't said anything.... Well, you see HE'S pretty quiet. And his brother's pretty quiet, and them four witnesses that lied so and got paid for it, they're pretty quiet. And as for Uncle Silas, it ain't any use for him to put in his oar, I wouldn't believe him under oath!"

Well, sir, that fairly made them shout; and even the judge he let go and laughed. Tom he was just feeling like a rainbow. When they was done laughing he looks up at the judge and says:

"Your honor, there's a thief in this house."

"A thief?"

"Yes, sir. And he's got them twelve-thousand-dollar di'monds on him."

By gracious, but it made a stir! Everybody went shouting:

"Which is him? Which is him? P'int him out!"

And the judge says:

"Point him out, my lad. Sheriff, you will arrest him. Which one is it?"

Tom says:

"This late dead man here — Jubiter Dunlap."

Then there was another thundering let-go of astonishment and excitement; but Jubiter, which was astonished enough before, was just fairly putrified with astonishment this time. And he spoke up, about half crying, and says:

"Now THAT'S a lie. Your honor, it ain't fair; I'm plenty bad enough without that. I done the other things — Brace he put me up to it, and persuaded me, and promised he'd make me rich, some day, and I done it, and I'm sorry I done it, and I wisht I hadn't; but I hain't stole no di'monds, and I hain't GOT no di'monds; I wisht I may never stir if it ain't so. The sheriff can search me and see."

Tom says:

"Your honor, it wasn't right to call him a thief, and I'll let up on that a little. He did steal the di'monds, but he didn't know it. He stole them from his brother Jake when he was laying dead, after Jake had stole them from the other thieves; but Jubiter didn't know he was stealing them; and he's been swelling around here with them a month; yes, sir, twelve thousand dollars' worth of di'monds on him — all that riches, and going around here every day just like a poor man. Yes, your honor, he's got them on him now."

The judge spoke up and says:

"Search him, sheriff."

Well, sir, the sheriff he ransacked him high and low, and everywhere: searched his hat, socks, seams, boots, everything — and Tom he stood there quiet, laying for another of them effects of hisn. Finally the sheriff he give it up, and everybody looked disappointed, and Jubiter says:

"There, now! what'd I tell you?"

And the judge says:

"It appears you were mistaken this time, my boy."

Then Tom took an attitude and let on to be studying with all his might, and scratching his head. Then all of a sudden he glanced up chipper, and says:

"Oh, now I've got it! I'd forgot."

Which was a lie, and I knowed it. Then he says:

"Will somebody be good enough to lend me a little small screwdriver? There was one in your brother's hand-bag that you smouched, Jubiter, but I reckon you didn't fetch it with you."

"No, I didn't. I didn't want it, and I give it away."

"That's because you didn't know what it was for."

Jubiter had his boots on again, by now, and when the thing Tom wanted was passed over the people's heads till it got to him, he says to Jubiter:

"Put up your foot on this chair." And he kneeled down and begun to unscrew the heel-plate, everybody watching; and when he got that big di'mond out of that boot-heel and held it up and let it flash and blaze and squirt sunlight everwhichaway, it just took everybody's breath; and Jubiter he looked so sick and sorry you never see the like of it. And when Tom held up the other di'mond he looked sorrier than ever. Land! He was thinking how he would 'a' skipped out and been rich and independent in a foreign land if he'd only had the luck to guess what the screwdriver was in the carpet-bag for.

Well, it was a most exciting time, take it all around, and Tom got cords of glory. The judge took the di'monds, and stood up in his pulpit, and cleared his throat, and shoved his spectacles back on his head, and says:

"I'll keep them and notify the owners; and when they send for them it will be a real pleasure to me to hand you the two thousand dollars, for you've earned the money — yes, and you've earned the deepest and most sincerest thanks of this community besides, for lifting a wronged and innocent family out of ruin and shame, and saving a good and honorable man from a felon's death, and for exposing to infamy and the punishment of the law a cruel and odious scoundrel and his miserable creatures!"

Well, sir, if there'd been a brass band to bust out some music, then, it would 'a' been just the perfectest thing I ever see, and Tom Sawyer he said the same.

Then the sheriff he nabbed Brace Dunlap and his crowd, and by and by next month the judge had them up for trial and jailed the whole lot. And everybody crowded back to Uncle Silas's little old church, and was ever so loving and kind to him and the family and couldn't do enough for them; and Uncle Silas he preached them the blamedest jumbledest idiotic sermons you ever struck, and would tangle you up so you couldn't find your way home in daylight; but the people never let on but what they thought it was the clearest and brightest and elegantest sermons that ever was; and they would set there and cry, for love and pity; but, by George, they give me the jim-jams and the fan-tods and caked up what brains I had, and turned them solid; but by and by they loved the old man's intellects back into him again, and he was as sound in his skull as ever he was, which ain't no flattery, I reckon. And so the whole family was as happy as birds, and nobody could be gratefuler and lovinger than what they was to Tom Sawyer; and the same to me, though I hadn't done nothing. And when the two thousand dollars come, Tom give half of it to me, and never told anybody so, which didn't surprise me, because I knowed him.

The Stolen White Elephant

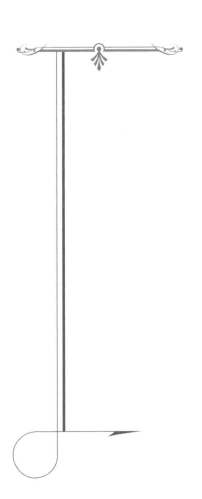

[*Left out of* A Tramp Abroad, *because it was feared that some of the particulars had been exaggerated, and that others were not true. Before these suspicions had been proven groundless, the book had gone to press.* — M. T.]

I.

*T*HE FOLLOWING CURIOUS HISTORY was related to me by a chance railway acquaintance. He was a gentleman more than seventy years of age, and his thoroughly good and gentle face and earnest and sincere manner imprinted the unmistakable stamp of truth upon every statement which fell from his lips. He said:

You know in what reverence the royal white elephant of Siam is held by the people of that country. You know it is sacred to kings, only kings may possess it, and that it is, indeed, in a measure even superior to kings, since it receives not merely honor but worship. Very well, five years ago, when the troubles concerning the frontier line arose between Great Britain and Siam, it was presently manifest that Siam had been in the wrong. Therefore every reparation was quickly made, and the British representative stated that he was satisfied and the past should be forgotten. This greatly relieved the King of Siam, and partly as a token of gratitude, partly also, perhaps, to wipe out any little remaining vestige of unpleasantness which England might feel toward him, he wished to send the Queen a present — the sole sure way of propitiating an enemy, according to Oriental ideas. This present ought not only to be a royal one, but transcendently royal. Wherefore, what offering could be so meet as that of a white elephant? My position in the Indian civil service was such that I was deemed peculiarly worthy of the honor of conveying the present to her Majesty. A ship was fitted out for me and my servants and the officers and attendants of the elephant, and in due time I arrived in New York harbor and placed my royal charge in admirable quarters in Jersey City. It was necessary to remain awhile in order to recruit the animal's health before resuming the voyage.

All went well during a fortnight — then my calamities began. The white elephant was stolen! I was called up at dead of night and informed of this fearful misfortune. For some moments I was beside myself with terror and anxiety; I was helpless. Then I grew calmer and collected my faculties. I soon saw my course — for, indeed, there was but the one course for an intelligent man to pursue. Late as it was, I flew to New York and got a policeman to conduct me to the headquarters of the detective force. Fortunately I arrived in time, though the chief of the force, the celebrated Inspector Blunt was just on the point of leaving for his home. He was a man of middle size and compact frame, and when he was thinking deeply he had a way of knitting his brows and tapping his forehead reflectively with his finger, which impressed you at once with the conviction that you stood in the presence of a person of no common order. The very sight of him gave me confidence and made me hopeful. I stated my errand. It did not flurry him in the least; it had no more visible effect upon his iron self-possession than if I had told him somebody had stolen my dog. He motioned me to a seat, and said, calmly:

"Allow me to think a moment, please."

So saying, he sat down at his office table and leaned his head upon his hand. Several clerks were at work at the other end of the room; the scratching of their pens was all the sound I heard during the next six or seven minutes. Meantime the inspector sat there, buried in thought. Finally he raised his head, and there was that in the firm lines of his face which showed me that his brain had done its work and his plan was made. Said he — and his voice was low and impressive:

"This is no ordinary case. Every step must be warily taken; each step must be made sure before the next is ventured. And secrecy must be observed — secrecy profound and absolute. Speak to no one about the matter, not even the reporters. I will take care of them; I will see that they get only what it may suit my ends to let them know." He touched a bell; a youth appeared. "Alaric, tell the reporters to remain for the present." The boy retired. "Now let us proceed to business — and systematically. Nothing can be accomplished in this trade of mine without strict and minute method."

He took a pen and some paper. "Now — name of the elephant?"

"Hassan Ben Ali Ben Selim Abdallah Mohammed Moist Alhammal Jamset-jejeebhoy Dhuleep Sultan Ebu Bhudpoor."

"Very well. Given name?"

"Jumbo."

"Very well. Place of birth?"

"The capital city of Siam."

"Parents living?"

"No — dead."

"Had they any other issue besides this one?"

"None. He was an only child."

"Very well. These matters are sufficient under that head. Now please describe the elephant, and leave out no particular, however insignificant — that is, insignificant from your point of view. To me in my profession there are no insignificant particulars; they do not exist."

I described, he wrote. When I was done, he said:

"Now listen. If I have made any mistakes, correct me."

He read as follows:

"Height, 19 feet; length from apex of forehead insertion of tail, 26 feet; length of trunk, 16 feet; length of tail, 6 feet; total length, including trunk, and tail, 48 feet; length of tusks, 9 feet; ears keeping with these dimensions; footprint resembles the mark left when one up-ends a barrel in the snow; the color of the elephant, a dull white; has a hole the size of a plate in each ear for the insertion of jewelry and possesses the habit in a remarkable degree of squirting water upon spectators and of maltreating with his trunk not only such persons as he is acquainted with, but even entire strangers; limps slightly with his right hind leg, and has a small scar in his left armpit caused by a former boil; had on, when stolen, a castle containing seats for fifteen persons, and a gold-cloth saddle-blanket the size of an ordinary carpet."

There were no mistakes. The inspector touched the bell, handed the description to Alaric, and said:

"Have fifty thousand copies of this printed at once and mailed to every detective office and pawnbroker's shop on the continent." Alaric retired. "There — so far, so good. Next, I must have a photograph of the property."

I gave him one. He examined it critically, and said:

"It must do, since we can do no better; but he has his trunk curled up and tucked into his mouth. That is unfortunate, and is calculated to mislead, for of course he does not usually have it in that position." He touched his bell.

"Alaric, have fifty thousand copies of this photograph made the first thing in the morning, and mail them with the descriptive circulars."

Alaric retired to execute his orders. The inspector said:

"It will be necessary to offer a reward, of course. Now as to the amount?"

"What sum would you suggest?"

"To begin with, I should say — well, twenty-five thousand dollars. It is an intricate and difficult business; there are a thousand avenues of escape and opportunities of concealment. These thieves have friends and pals everywhere — "

"Bless me, do you know who they are?"

The wary face, practised in concealing the thoughts and feelings within, gave me no token, nor yet the replying words, so quietly uttered:

"Never mind about that. I may, and I may not. We generally gather a pretty shrewd inkling of who our man is by the manner of his work and the size of the game he goes after. We are not dealing with a pickpocket or a hall thief now, make up your mind to that. This property was not 'lifted' by a novice. But, as I was saying, considering the amount of travel which will have to be done, and the diligence with which the thieves will cover up their traces as they move along, twenty-five thousand may be too small a sum to offer, yet I think it worth while to start with that."

So we determined upon that figure as a beginning. Then this man, whom nothing escaped which could by any possibility be made to serve as a clue, said:

"There are cases in detective history to show that criminals have been detected through peculiarities, in their appetites. Now, what does this elephant eat, and how much?"

"Well, as to what he eats — he will eat anything. He will eat a man, he will eat a Bible — he will eat anything between a man and a Bible."

"Good very good, indeed, but too general. Details are necessary — details are the only valuable things in our trade. Very well — as to men. At one meal — or, if you prefer, during one day — how many men will he eat, if fresh?"

"He would not care whether they were fresh or not; at a single meal he would eat five ordinary men."

"Very good; five men; we will put that down. What nationalities would he prefer?"

"He is indifferent about nationalities. He prefers acquaintances, but is not prejudiced against strangers."

"Very good. Now, as to Bibles. How many Bibles would he eat at a meal?"

"He would eat an entire edition."

"It is hardly succinct enough. Do you mean the ordinary octavo, or the family illustrated?"

"I think he would be indifferent to illustrations that is, I think he would not value illustrations above simple letterpress."

"No, you do not get my idea. I refer to bulk. The ordinary octavo Bible weighs about two pound and a half, while the great quarto with the illustrations weighs ten or twelve. How many Dore Bibles would he eat at a meal?"

"If you knew this elephant, you could not ask. He would take what they had."

"Well, put it in dollars and cents, then. We must get at it somehow. The Dore costs a hundred dollars a copy, Russia leather, beveled."

"He would require about fifty thousand dollars worth — say an edition of five hundred copies."

"Now that is more exact. I will put that down. Very well; he likes men and Bibles; so far, so good. What else will he eat? I want particulars."

"He will leave Bibles to eat bricks, he will leave bricks to eat bottles, he will leave bottles to eat clothing, he will leave clothing to eat cats, he will leave cats to eat oysters, he will leave oysters to eat ham, he will leave ham to eat sugar, he will leave sugar to eat pie, he will leave pie to eat potatoes, he will leave potatoes to eat bran; he will leave bran to eat hay, he will leave hay to eat oats, he will leave oats to eat rice, for he was mainly raised on it. There is nothing whatever that he will not eat but European butter, and he would eat that if he could taste it."

"Very good. General quantity at a meal — say about — "

"Well, anywhere from a quarter to half a ton."

"And he drinks — "

"Everything that is fluid. Milk, water, whisky, molasses, castor oil, camphene, carbolic acid — it is no use to go into particulars; whatever fluid occurs to you set it down. He will drink anything that is fluid, except European coffee."

"Very good. As to quantity?"

"Put it down five to fifteen barrels — his thirst varies; his other appetites do not."

"These things are unusual. They ought to furnish quite good clues toward tracing him."

He touched the bell.

"Alaric; summon Captain Burns."

Burns appeared. Inspector Blunt unfolded the whole matter to him, detail by detail. Then he said in the clear, decisive tones of a man whose plans are clearly defined in his head and who is accustomed to command:

"Captain Burns, detail Detectives Jones, Davis, Halsey, Bates, and Hackett to shadow the elephant."

"Yes, sir."

"Detail Detectives Moses, Dakin, Murphy, Rogers, Tupper, Higgins, and Bartholomew to shadow the thieves."

"Yes, sir."

"Place a strong guard — A guard of thirty picked men, with a relief of thirty — over the place from whence the elephant was stolen, to keep strict watch there night and day, and allow none to approach — except reporters — without written authority from me."

"Yes, sir."

"Place detectives in plain clothes in the railway; steamship, and ferry depots, and upon all roadways leading out of Jersey City, with orders to search all suspicious persons."

"Yes, sir."

"Furnish all these men with photograph and accompanying description of the elephant, and instruct them to search all trains and outgoing ferryboats and other vessels."

"Yes, sir."

"If the elephant should be found, let him be seized, and the information forwarded to me by telegraph."

"Yes, sir."

"Let me be informed at once if any clues should be found; footprints of the animal, or anything of that kind."

"Yes, sir."

"Get an order commanding the harbor police to patrol the frontages vigilantly."

"Yes, sir."

"Despatch detectives in plain clothes over all the railways, north as far as Canada, west as far as Ohio, south as far as Washington."

"Yes, sir."

"Place experts in all the telegraph offices to listen in to all messages; and let them require that all cipher despatches be interpreted to them."

"Yes, sir."

"Let all these things be done with the utmost's secrecy — mind, the most impenetrable secrecy."

"Yes, sir."

"Report to me promptly at the usual hour."

"Yes, Sir."

"Go!"

"Yes, sir."

He was gone.

Inspector Blunt was silent and thoughtful a moment, while the fire in his eye cooled down and faded out. Then he turned to me and said in a placid voice:

"I am not given to boasting, it is not my habit; but — we shall find the elephant."

I shook him warmly by the hand and thanked him; and I felt my thanks, too. The more I had seen of the man the more I liked him and the more I admired him and marveled over the mysterious wonders of his profession. Then we parted for the night, and I went home with a far happier heart than I had carried with me to his office.

II

NEXT MORNING it was all in the newspapers, in the minutest detail. It even had additions — consisting of Detective This, Detective That, and Detective The Other's "Theory" as to how the robbery was done, who the robbers were, and whither they had flown with their booty. There were eleven of these theories, and they covered all the possibilities; and this single fact shows what independent thinkers detectives are. No two theories were alike, or even much resembled each other, save in one striking particular, and in that one all the other eleven theories were absolutely agreed. That was, that although the rear of my building was torn out and the only door remained locked, the elephant had not been removed through the rent, but by some other (undiscovered) outlet. All agreed that the robbers had made that rent only to mislead the detectives. That never would have occurred to me or to any other layman, perhaps, but it had not deceived the detectives for a moment. Thus, what I had supposed was the only thing that had no mystery about it was in fact the very thing I had gone furthest astray in. The eleven theories all named the supposed robbers, but no two named the same robbers; the total number of suspected persons was thirty-seven. The various newspaper accounts all closed with the most important opinion of all — that of Chief Inspector Blunt. A portion of this statement read as follows:

The chief knows who the two principals are, namely, "Brick" Daffy and "Red" McFadden. Ten days before the robbery was achieved he was already aware that it was to be attempted, and had quietly proceeded to shadow these two noted villains; but unfortunately on the night in question their track was lost, and before it could be found again the bird was flown — that is, the elephant.

Daffy and McFadden are the boldest scoundrels in the profession; the chief has reasons for believing that they are the men who stole the stove out of the detective headquarters on a bitter night last winter — in consequence of which the chief and every detective present were in the hands of the physicians before morning, some with frozen feet, others with frozen fingers, ears, and other members.

When I read the first half of that I was more astonished than ever at the wonderful sagacity of this strange man. He not only saw everything in the present with a clear eye, but even the future could not be hidden from him. I was soon at his office, and said I could not help wishing he had had those men arrested, and so prevented the trouble and loss; but his reply was simple and unanswerable:

"It is not our province to prevent crime, but to punish it. We cannot punish it until it is committed."

I remarked that the secrecy with which we had begun had been marred by the newspapers; not only all our facts but all our plans and purposes had been revealed; even all the suspected persons had been named; these would doubtless disguise themselves now, or go into hiding.

"Let them. They will find that when I am ready for them my hand will descend upon them, in their secret places, as unerringly as the hand of fate. As to the newspapers, we must keep in with them. Fame, reputation, constant public mention — these are the detective's bread and butter. He must publish his facts, else he will be supposed to have none; he must publish his theory, for nothing is so strange or striking as a detective's theory, or brings him so much wonderful respect; we must publish our plans, for these the journals insist upon having, and we could not deny them without offending. We must constantly show the public what we are doing, or they will believe we are doing nothing. It is much pleasanter to have a newspaper say,

'Inspector Blunt's ingenious and extraordinary theory is as follows,' than to have it say some harsh thing, or, worse still, some sarcastic one."

"I see the force of what you say. But I noticed that in one part of your remarks in the papers this morning you refused to reveal your opinion upon a certain minor point."

"Yes, we always do that; it has a good effect. Besides, I had not formed any opinion on that point, anyway."

I deposited a considerable sum of money with the inspector, to meet current expenses, and sat down to wait for news. We were expecting the telegrams to begin to arrive at any moment now. Meantime I reread the newspapers and also our descriptive circular, and observed that our twenty-five thousand dollars reward seemed to be offered only to detectives. I said I thought it ought to be offered to anybody who would catch the elephant. The inspector said:

"It is the detectives who will find the elephant; hence the reward will go to the right place. If other people found the animal, it would only be by watching the detectives and taking advantage of clues and indications stolen from them, and that would entitle the detectives to the reward, after all. The proper office of a reward is to stimulate the men who deliver up their time and their trained sagacities to this sort of work, and not to confer benefits upon chance citizens who stumble upon a capture without having earned the benefits by their own merits and labors."

This was reasonable enough, certainly. Now the telegraphic machine in the corner began to click, and the following despatch was the result:

> FLOWER STATION, N. Y., 7.30 A.M.
> Have got a clue. Found a succession of deep tracks across a farm near here. Followed them two miles east without result; think elephant went west. Shall now shadow him in that direction.
> DARLEY, Detective.

"Darley's one of the best men on the force," said the inspector. "We shall hear from him again before long."

Telegram No. 2 came:

BARKER'S, N. J., 7.40 A.M.

Just arrived. Glass factory broken open here during night, and eight hundred bottles taken. Only water in large quantity near here is five miles distant. Shall strike for there. Elephant will be thirsty. Bottles were empty.

DARLEY, Detective.

"That promises well, too," said the inspector.

"I told you the creature's appetites would not be bad clues."

Telegram No. 3:

TAYLORVILLE, L. I. 8.15 A.M.

A haystack near here disappeared during night. Probably eaten. Have got a clue, and am off.

HUBBARD, Detective.

"How he does move around!" said the inspector "I knew we had a difficult job on hand, but we shall catch him yet."

FLOWER STATION, N. Y., 9 A.M.

Shadowed the tracks three miles westward. Large, deep, and ragged. Have just met a farmer who says they are not elephant-tracks. Says they are holes where he dug up saplings for shade-trees when ground was frozen last winter. Give me orders how to proceed.

DARLEY, Detective.

"Aha! a confederate of the thieves! The thing, grows warm," said the inspector. He dictated the following telegram to Darley:

Arrest the man and force him to name his pals. Continue to follow the tracks to the Pacific, if necessary.

Chief BLUNT.

Next telegram:

CONEY POINT, PA., 8.45 A.M.

Gas office broken open here during night and three months'
unpaid gas bills taken Have got a clue and am away.

MURPHY, Detective.

"Heavens!" said the inspector; "would he eat gas bills?"

"Through ignorance — yes; but they cannot support life. At least, unassisted."

Now came this exciting telegram:

IRONVILLE, N. Y., 9.30 A.M.

Just arrived. This village in consternation. Elephant passed
through here at five this morning. Some say he went east
some say west, some north, some south — but all say they
did not wait to notice, particularly. He killed a horse; have
secured a piece of it for a clue Killed it with his trunk; from
style of blow, think he struck it left-handed From position
in which horse lies, think elephant traveled northward
along line Berkley Railway. Has four and a half hours' start,
but I move on his track at once.

HAWES, Detective

I uttered exclamations of joy. The inspector was as self-contained as a
graven image. He calmly touched his bell.

"Alaric, send Captain Burns here."

Burns appeared.

"How many men are ready for instant orders?"

"Ninety-six, sir."

"Send them north at once. Let them concentrate along the line of the
Berkley road north of Ironville."

"Yes, sir."

"Let them conduct their movements with the utmost secrecy. As fast as
others are at liberty, hold them for orders."

"Yes, sir."

"Go!"

"Yes, sir."

Presently came another telegram:

> SAGE CORNERS, N. Y., 10.30.
>
> Just arrived. Elephant passed through here at 8.15. All escaped from the town but a policeman Apparently elephant did not strike at policeman, but at the lamp-post. Got both. I have secured a portion of the policeman as clue.
> STUMM, Detective.

"So the elephant has turned westward," said the inspector. "However, he will not escape, for my men are scattered all over that region."

The next telegram said:

> GLOVER'S, 11.15
>
> Just arrived. Village deserted, except sick and aged. Elephant passed through three-quarters of an hour ago. The anti-temperance mass-meeting was in session; he put his trunk in at a window and washed it out with water from cistern. Some swallowed it — since dead; several drowned. Detectives Cross and O'Shaughnessy were passing through town, but going south — so missed elephant. Whole region for many miles around in terror — people flying from their homes. Wherever they turn they meet elephant, and many are killed.
> BRANT, Detective.

I could have shed tears, this havoc so distressed me. But the inspector only said:

"You see — we are closing in on him. He feels our presence; he has turned eastward again."

Yet further troublous news was in store for us. The telegraph brought this:

HOGANSPORT, 12.19.

Just arrived. Elephant passed through half an hour ago, creating wildest fright and excitement. Elephant raged around streets; two plumbers going by, killed one — other escaped. Regret general.

O'FLAHERTY, Detective.

"Now he is right in the midst of my men," said the inspector. "Nothing can save him."

A succession of telegrams came from detectives who were scattered through New Jersey and Pennsylvania, and who were following clues consisting of ravaged barns, factories, and Sunday-school libraries, with high hopes-hopes amounting to certainties, indeed. The inspector said:

"I wish I could communicate with them and order them north, but that is impossible. A detective only visits a telegraph office to send his report; then he is off again, and you don't know where to put your hand on him."

Now came this despatch:

BRIDGEPORT, CT., 12.15.

Barnum offers rate of $4,000 a year for exclusive privilege of using elephant as traveling advertising medium from now till detectives find him Wants to paste circus-posters on him. Desires immediate answer.

BOGGS, Detective.

"That is perfectly absurd!" I exclaimed.

"Of course it is," said the inspector. "Evidently Mr. Barnum, who thinks he is so sharp, does not know me — but I know him."

Then he dictated this answer to the despatch:

Mr. Barnum's offer declined. Make it $7,000 or nothing.

Chief BLUNT.

"There. We shall not have to wait long for an answer. Mr. Barnum is not at home; he is in the telegraph office — it is his way when he has business on hand. Inside of three — "

Done. — P. T. BARNUM.

So interrupted the clicking telegraphic instrument. Before I could make a comment upon this extraordinary episode, the following despatch carried my thoughts into another and very distressing channel:

BOLIVIA, N. Y., 12.50.

Elephant arrived here from the south and passed through toward the forest at 11.50, dispersing a funeral on the way, and diminishing the mourners by two. Citizens fired some small cannon-balls into him, and they fled. Detective Burke and I arrived ten minutes later, from the north, but mistook some excavations for footprints, and so lost a good deal of time; but at last we struck the right trail and followed it to the woods. We then got down on our hands and knees and continued to keep a sharp eye on the track, and so shadowed it into the brush. Burke was in advance. Unfortunately the animal had stopped to rest; therefore, Burke having his head down, intent upon the track, butted up against the elephant's hind legs before he was aware of his vicinity. Burke instantly arose to his feet, seized the tail, and exclaimed joyfully, "I claim the re — " but got no further, for a single blow of the huge trunk laid the brave fellow's fragments low in death. I fled rearward, and the elephant turned and shadowed me to the edge of the wood, making tremendous speed, and I should inevitably have been lost, but that the remains of the funeral providentially intervened again and diverted his attention. I have just learned that nothing of that funeral is now left; but this is no loss, for there is abundance of material for another Meantime, the elephant has disappeared again.

MULROONEY, Detective.

We heard no news except from the diligent and confident detectives scattered about New Jersey, Pennsylvania, Delaware, and Virginia — who were all following fresh and encouraging clues — until shortly after 2 P.M., when this telegram came:

> BAXTER CENTER, 2.15.
>
> Elephant been here, plastered over with circus-bills, and broke up a revival, striking down and damaging many who were on the point of entering upon a better life. Citizens penned him up and established a guard. When Detective Brown and I arrived, some time after, we entered enclosure and proceeded to identify elephant by photograph and description. All masks tallied exactly except one, which we could not see — the boil-scar under armpit. To make sure, Brown crept under to look, and was immediately brained — that is, head crushed and destroyed, though nothing issued from debris. All fled so did elephant, striking right and left with much effect. He escaped, but left bold blood-track from cannon-wounds. Rediscover certain. He broke southward, through a dense forest.
>
> BRENT, Detective.

That was the last telegram. At nightfall a fog shut down which was so dense that objects but three feet away could not be discerned. This lasted all night. The ferry-boats and even the omnibuses had to stop running.

III

NEXT MORNING the papers were as full of detective theories as before; they had all our tragic facts in detail also, and a great many more which they had received from their telegraphic correspondents. Column after column was occupied, a third of its way down, with glaring head-lines, which it made my heart sick to read. Their general tone was like this:

> THE WHITE ELEPHANT AT LARGE! HE MOVES UPON HIS FATAL MARCH WHOLE VILLAGES DESERTED BY THEIR FRIGHT-STRICKEN OCCUPANTS! PALE TERROR GOES BEFORE HIM, DEATH AND DEVASTATION FOLLOW AFTER! AFTER THESE, THE DETECTIVES! BARNS DESTROYED, FACTORIES GUTTED, HARVESTS DEVOURED, PUBLIC ASSEMBLAGES DISPERSED, ACCOMPANIED BY SCENES OF CARNAGE IMPOSSIBLE TO DESCRIBE! THEORIES OF THIRTY-FOUR OF THE MOST DISTINGUISHED DETECTIVES ON THE FORCES! THEORY OF CHIEF BLUNT!

"There!" said Inspector Blunt, almost betrayed into excitement, "this is magnificent! This is the greatest windfall that any detective organization ever had. The fame of it will travel to the ends of the earth, and endure to the end of time, and my name with it."

But there was no joy for me. I felt as if I had committed all those red crimes, and that the elephant was only my irresponsible agent. And how the list had grown! In one place he had "interfered with an election and killed five repeaters." He had followed this act with the destruction of two pool fellows, named O'Donohue and McFlannigan, who had "found a refuge in the home of the oppressed of all lands only the day before, and were in the act of exercising for the first time the noble right of American citizens at the polls, when stricken down by the relentless hand of the Scourge of Siam." In another, he had "found a crazy sensation-preacher preparing his next season's heroic attacks on the dance, the theater, and other things which can't strike back, and had stepped on him." And in still another place he had "killed a lightning-rod agent." And so the list went on, growing redder and redder, and more and more heartbreaking. Sixty persons had been killed, and two hundred and forty wounded. All the accounts bore just testimony to the activity and devotion of the detectives, and all closed with the remark that "three hundred thousand citizens; and four detectives saw the dread creature, and two of the latter he destroyed."

I dreaded to hear the telegraphic instrument begin to click again. By and by the messages began to pour in, but I was happily disappointed in their nature. It was soon apparent that all trace of the elephant was lost. The fog had enabled him to search out a good hiding-place unobserved. Telegrams from the most absurdly distant points reported that a dim vast mass had been glimpsed there through the fog at such and such an hour, and was "undoubtedly the elephant." This dim vast mass had been glimpsed in New Haven, in New Jersey, in Pennsylvania, in interior New York, in Brooklyn, and even in the city of New York itself! But in all cases the dim vast mass had vanished quickly and left no trace. Every detective of the large force scattered over this huge extent of country sent his hourly report, and each and every one of them had a clue, and was shadowing something, and was hot upon the heels of it.

But the day passed without other result.

The next day the same.

The next just the same.

The newspaper reports began to grow monotonous with facts that amounted to nothing, clues which led to nothing, and theories which had nearly exhausted the elements which surprise and delight and dazzle.

By advice of the inspector I doubled the reward.

Four more dull days followed. Then came a bitter blow to the poor, hard-working detectives — the journalists declined to print their theories, and coldly said, "Give us a rest."

Two weeks after the elephant's disappearance I raised the reward to seventy-five thousand dollars by the inspector's advice. It was a great sum, but I felt that I would rather sacrifice my whole private fortune than lose my credit with my government. Now that the detectives were in adversity, the newspapers turned upon them, and began to fling the most stinging sarcasms at them. This gave the minstrels an idea, and they dressed themselves as detectives and hunted the elephant on the stage in the most extravagant way. The caricaturists made pictures of detectives scanning the country with spy-glasses, while the elephant, at their backs, stole apples out of their pockets. And they made all sorts of ridiculous pictures of the detective badge — you have seen that badge printed in gold on the back of detective novels, no doubt it is a wide-staring eye, with the legend, "WE NEVER SLEEP." When detectives called for a drink, the would-be facetious barkeeper resurrected an obsolete form of expression and said, "Will you have an eye-opener?" All the air was thick with sarcasms.

But there was one man who moved calm, untouched, unaffected, through it all. It was that heart of oak, the chief inspector. His brave eye never drooped, his serene confidence never wavered. He always said:

"Let them rail on; he laughs best who laughs last."

My admiration for the man grew into a species of worship. I was at his side always. His office had become an unpleasant place to me, and now became daily more and more so. Yet if he could endure it I meant to do so also — at least, as long as I could. So I came regularly, and stayed — the only outsider who seemed to be capable of it. Everybody wondered how I could; and often it seemed to me that I must desert, but at such times I looked into that calm and apparently unconscious face, and held my ground.

About three weeks after the elephant's disappearance I was about to say, one morning, that I should have to strike my colors and retire, when the great detective arrested the thought by proposing one more superb and masterly move.

This was to compromise with the robbers. The fertility of this man's invention exceeded anything I have ever seen, and I have had a wide intercourse with the world's finest minds. He said he was confident he could compromise for one hundred thousand dollars and recover the elephant. I said I believed I could scrape the amount together, but what would become of the poor detectives who had worked so faithfully? He said:

"In compromises they always get half."

This removed my only objection. So the inspector wrote two notes, in this form:

> DEAR MADAM, — Your husband can make a large sum of money (and be entirely protected from the law) by making an immediate, appointment with me.
> Chief BLUNT.

He sent one of these by his confidential messenger to the "reputed wife" of Brick Duffy, and the other to the reputed wife of Red McFadden.

Within the hour these offensive answers came:

> YE OWLD FOOL: brick Duffys bin ded 2 yere.
> BRIDGET MAHONEY.
> CHIEF BAT, — Red McFadden is hung and in heving 18 month. Any Ass but a detective know that.
> MARY O'HOOLIGAN.

"I had long suspected these facts," said the inspector; "this testimony proves the unerring accuracy of my instinct."

The moment one resource failed him he was ready with another. He imme-diately wrote an advertisement for the morning papers, and I kept a copy of it:

> *A. — xWhlv. 242 ht. Tjnd — fz328wmlg. Ozpo, — 2 m!*
> *2m!. M! ogw.*

He said that if the thief was alive this would bring him to the usual ren-dezvous. He further explained that the usual rendezvous was a glare where all business affairs between detectives and criminals were conducted. This meeting would take place at twelve the next night.

We could do nothing till then, and I lost no time in getting out of the office, and was grateful indeed for the privilege.

At eleven the next night I brought one hundred thousand dollars in bank-notes and put them into the chief's hands, and shortly afterward he took his leave, with the brave old undimmed confidence in his eye. An almost intolerable hour dragged to a close; then I heard his welcome tread, and rose gasping and tottered to meet him. How his fine eyes flamed with triumph! He said:

"We've compromised! The jokers will sing a different tune to-morrow! Follow me!"

He took a lighted candle and strode down into the vast vaulted basement where sixty detectives always slept, and where a score were now playing cards to while the time. I followed close after him. He walked swiftly down to the dim and remote end of the place, and just as I succumbed to the pangs of suffocation and was swooning away he stumbled and fell over the outlying members of a mighty object, and I heard him exclaim as he went down:

"Our noble profession is vindicated. Here is your elephant!"

I was carried to the office above and restored with carbolic acid. The whole detective force swarmed in, and such another season of triumphant rejoicing ensued as I had never witnessed before. The reporters were called, baskets of champagne were opened, toasts were drunk, the handshakings and congratulations were continuous and enthusiastic. Naturally the chief was the hero of the hour, and his happiness was so complete and had been so patiently and worthily and bravely won that it made me happy to see it, though I stood there a homeless beggar, my priceless charge dead, and my position in my country's service lost to me through what would always seem my fatally careless execution of a great trust. Many an eloquent eye testified its deep admiration for the chief, and many a detective's voice murmured, "Look at him — just the king of the profession; only give him a clue, it's all he wants, and there ain't anything hid that he can't find." The dividing of the fifty thousand dollars made great pleasure; when it was finished the chief made a little speech while he put his share in his pocket, in which he said, "Enjoy it, boys, for you've earned it; and, more than that, you've earned for the detective profession undying fame."

A telegram arrived, which read:

> MONROE, MICH., 10 P.M.
> First time I've struck a telegraph office in over three weeks. Have followed those footprints, horseback, through the woods, a thousand miles to here, and they get stronger and bigger and fresher every day. Don't worry-inside of another week I'll have the elephant. This is dead sure.
> DARLEY, Detective.

The chief ordered three cheers for "Darley, one of the finest minds on the force," and then commanded that he be telegraphed to come home and receive his share of the reward.

So ended that marvelous episode of the stolen elephant. The newspapers were pleasant with praises once more, the next day, with one contemptible exception. This sheet said, "Great is the detective! He may be a little slow in finding a little thing like a mislaid elephant; he may hunt him all day and sleep with his rotting carcass all night for three weeks, but he will find him at last if he can get the man who mislaid him to show him the place!"

Poor Hassan was lost to me forever. The cannonshots had wounded him fatally, he had crept to that unfriendly place in the fog, and there, surrounded by his enemies and in constant danger of detection, he had wasted away with hunger and suffering till death gave him peace.

The compromise cost me one hundred thousand dollars; my detective expenses were forty-two thousand dollars more; I never applied for a place again under my government; I am a ruined man and a wanderer on the earth but my admiration for that man, whom I believe to be the greatest detective the world has ever produced, remains undimmed to this day, and will so remain unto the end.

A Double Barrelled Detective Story

PART I

"We ought never to do wrong when people are looking."

I

THE FIRST SCENE is in the country, in Virginia, the time, 1880. There has been a wedding, between a handsome young man of slender means and a rich young girl — a case of love at first sight and a precipitate marriage; a marriage bitterly opposed by the girl's widowed father.

Jacob Fuller, the bridegroom, is twenty-six years old, is of an old but unconsidered family which had by compulsion emigrated from Sedgemoor, and for King James's purse's profit, so everybody said — some maliciously, the rest merely because they believed it. The bride is nineteen and beautiful. She is intense, high-strung, romantic, immeasurably proud of her Cavalier blood, and passionate in her love for her young husband. For its sake she braved her father's displeasure, endured his reproaches, listened with loyalty unshaken to his warning predictions, and went from his house without his blessing, proud and happy in the proofs she was thus giving of the quality of the affection which had made its home in her heart.

The morning after the marriage there was a sad surprise for her. Her husband put aside her proffered caresses, and said:

"Sit down. I have something to say to you. I loved you. That was before I asked your father to give you to me. His refusal is not my grievance — I could have endured that. But the things he said of me to you — that is a different matter. There — you needn't speak; I know quite well what they were; I got them from authentic sources. Among other things he said that my character was written in my face; that I was treacherous, a dissembler, a coward, and a brute without sense of pity or compassion: the 'Sedgemoor trade-mark,' he called it — and 'white-sleeve badge.' Any other man in my place would have gone to his house and shot him down like a dog. I wanted to do it, and was minded to do it, but a better thought came to me: to put him to shame; to break his heart, to kill him by inches. How to do it? Through my treatment of you, his idol! I would marry you; and then — Have patience. You will see."

From that moment onward, for three months, the young wife suffered all the humiliations, all the insults, all the miseries that the diligent and inventive mind of the husband could contrive, save physical injuries only. Her strong pride stood by her, and she kept the secret of her troubles. Now and then the husband said, "Why don't you go to your father and tell him?" Then he invented new tortures, applied them, and asked again. She always answered, "He shall never know by my mouth," and taunted him with his origin; said she was the lawful slave of a scion of slaves, and must obey, and would — up to that point, but no further; he could kill her if he liked, but he could not break her; it was not in the Sedgemoor breed to do it. At the end of the three months he said, with a dark significance in his manner, "I have tried all things but one" — and waited for her reply. "Try that," she said, and curled her lip in mockery.

That night he rose at midnight and put on his clothes, then said to her, "Get up and dress!"

She obeyed — as always, without a word. He led her half a mile from the house, and proceeded to lash her to a tree by the side of the public road; and succeeded, she screaming and struggling. He gagged her then, struck her across the face with his cowhide, and set his bloodhounds on her. They tore the clothes off her, and she was naked. He called the dogs off, and said:

"You will be found — by the passing public. They will be dropping along about three hours from now, and will spread the news — do you hear? Good-by. You have seen the last of me."

He went away then. She moaned to herself:

"I shall bear a child — to him! God grant it may be a boy!"

The farmers released her by-and-by — and spread the news, which was natural. They raised the country with lynching intentions, but the bird had flown. The young wife shut herself up in her father's house; he shut himself up with her, and thenceforth would see no one. His pride was broken, and his heart; so he wasted away, day by day, and even his daughter rejoiced when death relieved him.

Then she sold the estate and disappeared.

II

IN 1886 A YOUNG WOMAN was living in a modest house near a secluded New England village, with no company but a little boy about five years old. She did her own work, she discouraged acquaintanceships, and had none. The butcher, the baker, and the others who served her could tell the villagers nothing about her further than that her name was Stillman, and that she called the child Archy. Whence she came they had not been able to find out, but they said she talked like a Southerner. The child had no playmates and no comrade, and no teacher but the mother. She taught him diligently and intelligently, and was satisfied with the results — even a little proud of them. One day Archy said,

"Mamma, am I different from other children?"

"Well, I suppose not. Why?"

"There was a child going along out there and asked me if the postman had been by and I said yes, and she said how long since I saw him and I said I hadn't seen him at all, and she said how did I know he'd been by, then, and I said because I smelt his track on the sidewalk, and she said I was a dumb fool and made a mouth at me. What did she do that for?"

The young woman turned white, and said to herself, "It's a birthmark! The gift of the bloodhound is in him." She snatched the boy to her breast and hugged him passionately, saying, "God has appointed the way!" Her eyes were burning with a fierce light, and her breath came short and quick with excitement. She said to herself: "The puzzle is solved now; many a time it has been a mystery to me, the impossible things the child has done in the dark, but it is all clear to me now."

She set him in his small chair, and said,

"Wait a little till I come, dear; then we will talk about the matter."

She went up to her room and took from her dressing-table several small articles and put them out of sight: a nail-file on the floor under the bed; a pair of nail-scissors under the bureau; a small ivory paper-knife under the wardrobe. Then she returned, and said,

"There! I have left some things which I ought to have brought down." She named them, and said, "Run up and bring them, dear."

The child hurried away on his errand and was soon back again with the things.

"Did you have any difficulty, dear?"

"No, mamma; I only went where you went."

During his absence she had stepped to the bookcase, taken several books from the bottom shelf, opened each, passed her hand over a page, noting its number in her memory, then restored them to their places. Now she said:

"I have been doing something while you have been gone, Archy. Do you think you can find out what it was?"

The boy went to the bookcase and got out the books that had been touched, and opened them at the pages which had been stroked.

The mother took him in her lap, and said,

"I will answer your question now, dear. I have found out that in one way you are quite different from other people. You can see in the dark, you can smell what other people cannot, you have the talents of a bloodhound. They are good and valuable things to have, but you must keep the matter a secret. If people found it out, they would speak of you as an odd child, a strange child, and children would be disagreeable to you, and give you nicknames. In this world one must be like everybody else if he doesn't want to provoke scorn or envy or jealousy. It is a great and fine distinction which has been born to you, and I am glad; but you will keep it a secret, for mamma's sake, won't you?"

The child promised, without understanding.

All the rest of the day the mother's brain was busy with excited thinkings; with plans, projects, schemes, each and all of them uncanny, grim, and dark. Yet they lit up her face; lit it with a fell light of their own; lit it with vague fires of hell. She was in a fever of unrest; she could not sit, stand, read, sew; there was no relief for her but in movement. She tested her boy's gift in twenty ways, and kept saying to herself all the time, with her mind in the past: "He broke my father's heart, and night and day all these years I have tried, and all in vain, to think out a way to break his. I have found it now — I have found it now."

When night fell, the demon of unrest still possessed her. She went on with her tests; with a candle she traversed the house from garret to cellar, hiding pins, needles, thimbles, spools, under pillows, under carpets, in cracks in the walls, under the coal in the bin; then sent the little fellow in the dark to find them; which he did, and was happy and proud when she praised him and smothered him with caresses.

From this time forward life took on a new complexion for her. She said, "The future is secure — I can wait, and enjoy the waiting." The most of her lost interests revived. She took up music again, and languages, drawing, painting, and the other long-discarded delights of her maidenhood. She was happy once more, and felt again the zest of life. As the years drifted by she watched the development of her boy, and was contented with it. Not altogether, but nearly that. The soft side of his heart was larger than the other side of it. It was his only defect, in her eyes. But she considered that his love for her and worship of her made up for it. He was a good hater — that was well; but it was a question if the materials of his hatreds were of as tough and enduring a quality as those of his friendships — and that was not so well.

The years drifted on. Archy was become a handsome, shapely, athletic youth, courteous, dignified, companionable, pleasant in his ways, and looking perhaps a trifle older than he was, which was sixteen. One evening his mother said she had something of grave importance to say to him, adding that he was old enough to hear it now, and old enough and possessed of character enough and stability enough to carry out a stern plan which she had been for years contriving and maturing. Then she told him her bitter story, in all its naked atrociousness. For a while the boy was paralyzed; then he said,

"I understand. We are Southerners; and by our custom and nature there is but one atonement. I will search him out and kill him."

"Kill him? No! Death is release, emancipation; death is a favor. Do I owe him favors? You must not hurt a hair of his head."

The boy was lost in thought awhile; then he said,

"You are all the world to me, and your desire is my law and my pleasure. Tell me what to do and I will do it."

The mother's eyes beamed with satisfaction, and she said,

"You will go and find him. I have known his hiding-place for eleven years; it cost me five years and more of inquiry, and much money, to locate it. He is a quartz-miner in Colorado, and well-to-do. He lives in Denver. His name is Jacob Fuller. There — it is the first time I have spoken it since that unforgettable night. Think! That name could have been yours if I had not saved you that shame and furnished you a cleaner one. You will drive him from that place; you will hunt him down and drive him again; and yet again, and again, and again, persistently, relentlessly, poisoning his life, filling it with mysterious terrors, loading it with weariness and misery, making him wish for death, and that he had a suicide's courage; you will make of him another Wandering Jew; he shall know no rest any more, no peace of mind, no placid sleep; you shall shadow him, cling to him, persecute him, till you break his heart, as he broke my father's and mine."

"I will obey, mother."

"I believe it, my child. The preparations are all made; everything is ready. Here is a letter of credit; spend freely, there is no lack of money. At times you may need disguises. I have provided them; also some other conveniences." She took from the drawer of the type-writer-table several squares of paper. They all bore these typewritten words:

$10,000 REWARD

It is believed that a certain man who is wanted in an Eastern state is sojourning here. In 1880, in the night, he tied his young wife to a tree by the public road, cut her across the face with a cowhide, and made his dogs tear her clothes from her, leaving her naked. He left her there, and fled the country. A blood-relative of hers has searched for him for seventeen years. Address... ......,........., Post-office. The above reward will be paid in cash to the person who will furnish the seeker, in a personal interview, the criminal's address.

"When you have found him and acquainted yourself with his scent, you will go in the night and placard one of these upon the building he occupies, and another one upon the post-office or in some other prominent place. It will be the talk of the region. At first you must give him several days in which to force a sale of his belongings at something approaching their value. We will ruin him by-and-by, but gradually; we must not impoverish him at once, for that could bring him to despair and injure his health, possibly kill him."

She took three or four more typewritten forms from the drawer — duplicates — and read one:

........,........., 18...

To Jacob Fuller:

You have...... days in which to settle your affairs. You will not

be disturbed during that limit, which will expire at. ..... M., on the...... of....... You must then MOVE ON. If you are still in the place after the named hour, I will placard you on all the dead walls, detailing your crime once more, and adding the date, also the scene of it, with all names concerned, including your own. Have no fear of bodily injury — it will in no circumstances ever be inflicted upon you. You brought misery upon an old man, and ruined his life and broke his heart. What he suffered, you are to suffer. "You will add no signature. He must receive this before he learns of the reward-placard — before he rises in the morning — lest he lose his head and fly the place penniless."

"I shall not forget."

"You will need to use these forms only in the beginning — once may be enough. Afterward, when you are ready for him to vanish out of a place, see that he gets a copy of this form, which merely says,

MOVE ON. You have...... days.

"He will obey. That is sure."

III

EXTRACTS FROM LETTERS TO THE MOTHER:

DENVER, April 3, 1897.

I have now been living several days in the same hotel with Jacob Fuller. I have his scent; I could track him through ten divisions of infantry and find him. I have often been near him and heard him talk. He owns a good mine, and has a fair income from it; but he is not rich. He learned mining in a good way —

by working at it for wages. He is a cheerful creature, and his forty-three years sit lightly upon him; he could pass for a younger man — say thirty-six or thirty-seven. He has never married again — passes himself off for a widower. He stands well, is liked, is popular, and has many friends. Even I feel a drawing toward him — the paternal blood in me making its claim. How blind and unreasoning and arbitrary are some of the laws of nature — the most of them, in fact! My task is become hard now — you realize it? You comprehend, and make allowances — and the fire of it has cooled, more than I like to confess to myself. But I will carry it out. Even with the pleasure paled, the duty remains, and I will not spare him.

And for my help, a sharp resentment rises in me when I reflect that he who committed that odious crime is the only one who has not suffered by it. The lesson of it has manifestly reformed his character, and in the change he is happy. He, the guilty party, is absolved from all suffering; you, the innocent, are borne down with it. But be comforted — he shall harvest his share.

SILVER GULCH, May 19.

I placarded Form No. 1 at midnight of April 3; an hour later I slipped Form No. 2 under his chamber door, notifying him to leave Denver at or before 11.50 the night of the 14th.

Some late bird of a reporter stole one of my placards, then hunted the town over and found the other one, and stole that. In this manner he accomplished what the profession calls a "scoop" — that is, he got a valuable item, and saw to it that no other paper got it. And so his paper — the principal one in the town — had it in glaring type on the editorial page in the morning, followed by a Vesuvian opinion of our wretch a column long, which wound up by adding a thousand dollars to our reward on the paper's account! The journals out here know how to do the noble thing — when there's business in it.

At breakfast I occupied my usual seat — selected because it afforded a view of papa Fuller's face, and was near enough for me to hear the talk that went on at his table. Seventy-five or a hundred people were in the room, and all discussing that item, and saying they hoped the seeker would find that rascal and remove the pollution of his presence from the town — with a rail, or a bullet, or something.

When Fuller came in he had the Notice to Leave — folded up — in one hand, and the newspaper in the other; and it gave me more than half a pang to see him. His cheerfulness was all gone, and he looked old and pinched and ashy. And then — only think of the things he had to listen to! Mamma, he heard his own unsuspecting friends describe him with epithets and characterizations drawn from the very dictionaries and phrase-books of Satan's own authorized editions down below. And more than that, he had to agree with the verdicts and applaud them. His applause tasted bitter in his mouth, though; he could not disguise that from me; and it was observable that his appetite was gone; he only nibbled; he couldn't eat. Finally a man said,

"It is quite likely that that relative is in the room and hearing what this town thinks of that unspeakable scoundrel. I hope so."

Ah, dear, it was pitiful the way Fuller winced, and glanced around scared! He couldn't endure any more, and got up and left.

During several days he gave out that he had bought a mine in Mexico, and wanted to sell out and go down there as soon as he could, and give the property his personal attention. He played his cards well; said he would take $40,000 — a quarter in cash, the rest in safe notes; but that as he greatly needed money on account of his new purchase, he would diminish his terms for cash in full, He sold out for $30,000. And then, what do you think he did? He asked for greenbacks, and took them, saying the man in Mexico was a New-Englander, with a head full of crotchets, and preferred greenbacks to gold or drafts. People thought it queer, since a draft on New York could produce greenbacks quite conveniently. There was talk of this odd thing, but only for a day; that is as long as any topic lasts in Denver.

I was watching, all the time. As soon as the sale was completed and the money paid — which was on the 11th — I began to stick to Fuller's track without dropping it for a moment. That night — no, 12th, for it was a little past midnight — I tracked him to his room, which was four doors from mine in the same hall; then I went back and put on my muddy day-laborer disguise, darkened my complexion, and sat down in my room in the gloom, with a gripsack handy, with a change in it, and my door ajar. For I suspected that the bird would take wing now. In half an hour an old woman passed by, carrying a grip; I caught the familiar whiff, and followed with my grip, for it was Fuller. He left the hotel by a side entrance, and at the corner he turned up an unfrequented street and walked three blocks in a light rain and a heavy darkness, and got into a two-horse hack, which, of course, was waiting for him by appointment. I took a seat (uninvited) on the trunk platform behind, and we drove briskly off. We drove ten miles, and the hack stopped at a way station and was discharged. Fuller got out and took a seat on a barrow under the awning, as far as he could get from the light; I went inside, and watched the ticket-office. Fuller bought no ticket; I bought none. Presently the train came along, and he boarded a car; I entered the same car at the other end, and came down the aisle and took the seat behind him. When he paid the conductor and named his objective point, I dropped back several seats, while the conductor was changing a bill, and when he came to me I paid to the same place — about a hundred miles westward.

From that time for a week on end he led me a dance. He travelled here and there and yonder — always on a general westward trend — but he was not a woman after the first day. He was a laborer, like myself, and wore bushy false whiskers. His outfit was perfect, and he could do the character without thinking about it, for he had served the trade for wages. His nearest friend could not have recognized him. At last he located himself here, the obscurest little mountain camp in Montana; he has a shanty, and goes out prospecting daily; is gone all day, and avoids society. I am living at a miner's boarding-house, and it is an awful place: the bunks, the food, the dirt — everything.

We have been here four weeks, and in that time I have seen him but once; but every night I go over his track and post myself. As soon as he engaged a shanty here I went to a town fifty miles away and telegraphed that Denver hotel to keep my baggage till I should send for it. I need nothing here but a change of army shirts, and I brought that with me.

SILVER GULCH, June 12.

The Denver episode has never found its way here, I think. I know most of the men in camp, and they have never referred to it, at least in my hearing. Fuller doubtless feels quite safe in these conditions. He has located a claim, two miles away, in an out-of-the-way place in the mountains; it promises very well, and he is working it diligently. Ah, but the change in him! He never smiles, and he keeps quite to himself, consorting with no one — he who was so fond of company and so cheery only two months ago. I have seen him passing along several times recently — drooping, forlorn, the spring gone from his step, a pathetic figure. He calls himself David Wilson.

I can trust him to remain here until we disturb him. Since you insist, I will banish him again, but I do not see how he can be unhappier than he already is. I will go hack to Denver and treat myself to a little season of comfort, and edible food, and endurable beds, and bodily decency; then I will fetch my things, and notify poor papa Wilson to move on.

DENVER, June 19.

They miss him here. They all hope he is prospering in Mexico, and they do not say it just with their mouths, but out of their hearts. You know you can always tell. I am loitering here overlong, I confess it. But if you were in my place you would have charity for me. Yes, I know what you will say, and you are right: if I were in your place, and carried your scalding memories in my heart —

I will take the night train back to-morrow.

DENVER, June 20.

God forgive us, mother, we are hunting the wrong man! I have not slept any all night. I am now awaiting, at dawn, for the morning train — and how the minutes drag, how they drag!

This Jacob Fuller is a cousin of the guilty one. How stupid we have been not to reflect that the guilty one would never again wear his own name after that fiendish deed! The Denver Fuller is four years younger than the other one; he came here a young widower in '79, aged twenty-one — a year before you were married; and the documents to prove it are innumerable. Last night I talked with familiar friends of his who have known him from the day of his arrival. I said nothing, but a few days from now I will land him in this town again, with the loss upon his mine made good; and there will be a banquet, and a torch-light procession, and there will not be any expense on anybody but me. Do you call this "gush"? I am only a boy, as you well know; it is my privilege. By-and-by I shall not be a boy any more.

SILVER GULCH, July 3.

Mother, he is gone! Gone, and left no trace. The scent was cold when I came. Today I am out of bed for the first time since. I wish I were not a boy; then I could stand shocks better. They all think he went west. I start tonight, in a wagon — two or three hours of that, then I get a train. I don't know where I'm going, but I must go; to try to keep still would be torture.

Of course he has effaced himself with a new name and a disguise. This means that I may have to search the whole globe to find him. Indeed it is what I expect. Do you see, mother? It is I that am the Wandering Jew. The irony of it! We arranged that for another.

Think of the difficulties! And there would be none if I only could advertise for him. But if there is any way to do it that would not frighten him, I have not been able to think it out, and I have tried till my brains are addled. "If the gentleman who lately bought a mine in Mexico and sold one in Denver will send his address to — " (to whom, mother?), "it will be explained to him that it was all a mistake; his forgiveness will be asked, and full reparation made for a loss which he sustained in a certain matter." Do you see? He would think it a trap. Well, any one would. If I should say, "It is now known that he was not the man wanted, but another man — a man who once bore the same name, but discarded it for good reasons" — would that answer? But the Denver people would wake up then and say "Oho!" and they would remember about the suspicious greenbacks, and say, "Why did he run away if he wasn't the right man? — It is too thin." If I failed to find him he would be ruined there — there where there is no taint upon him now. You have a better head than mine. Help me.

I have one clue, and only one. I know his handwriting. If he puts his new false name upon a hotel register and does not disguise it too much, it will be valuable to me if I ever run across it.

SAN FRANCISCO, June 28, 1898.

You already know how well I have searched the states from Colorado to the Pacific, and how nearly I came to getting him once. Well, I have had another close miss. It was here, yesterday. I struck his trail, hot, on the street, and followed it on a run to a cheap hotel. That was a costly mistake; a dog would have gone the other way. But I am only part dog, and can get very humanly stupid when excited. He had been stopping in that house ten days; I almost know, now, that he stops long nowhere, the past six or eight months, but is restless and has to keep moving. I understand that feeling! And I know what it is to feel it. He still uses the name he had registered when I came so near catching him nine months ago — "James Walker;" doubtless the same he adopted when he fled from Silver Gulch. An unpretending man, and has small taste for fancy names. I recognized the hand easily, through its slight disguise. A square man, and not good at shams and pretenses.

They said he was just gone on a journey; left no address; didn't say where he was going; looked frightened when asked to leave his address; had no baggage but a cheap valise; carried it off on foot —

a "stingy old person, and not much loss to the house." "Old!" I suppose he is, now. I hardly heard; I was there but a moment. I rushed along his trail, and it led me to a wharf. Mother, the smoke of the steamer he had taken was just fading out on the horizon! I should have saved half an hour if I had gone in the right direction at first. I could have taken a fast tug, and should have stood a chance of catching that vessel. She is bound for Melbourne.

HOPE CANYON, CALIFORNIA, October 3, 1900.

You have a right to complain. "A letter a year" is a paucity; I freely acknowledge it; but how can one write when there is nothing to write about but failures? No one can keep it up; it breaks the heart.

I told you — it seems ages ago, now — how I missed him at Melbourne, and then chased him all over Australasia for months on end.

Well, then, after that I followed him to India; almost saw him in Bombay; traced him all around — to Baroda, Rawal-Pindi, Lucknow, Lahore, Cawnpore, Allahabad, Calcutta, Madras — oh, everywhere; week after week, month after month, through the dust and swelter — always approximately on his track, sometimes close upon him, yet never catching him. And down to Ceylon, and then to — Never mind; by-and-by I will write it all out.

I chased him home to California, and down to Mexico, and back again to California. Since then I have been hunting him about the state from the first of last January down to a month ago. I feel almost sure he is not far from Hope Canyon; I traced him to a point thirty miles from here, but there I lost the trail; some one gave him a lift in a wagon, I suppose.

I am taking a rest, now — modified by searchings for the lost trail. I was tired to death, mother, and low-spirited, and sometimes coming uncomfortably near to losing hope; but the miners in this little camp are good fellows, and I am used to their sort this long time back; and their breezy ways freshen a person up and make him forget his troubles. I have been here a month. I am cabining with a young fellow named "Sammy" Hillyer, about twenty-five, the only son of his mother — like me — and loves her dearly, and writes to her every week — part of which is like me. He is a timid body, and in the matter of intellect — well, he cannot be depended upon to set a river on fire; but no matter, he is well liked; he is good and fine, and it is meat and bread and rest and luxury to sit and talk with him and have a comradeship again. I wish "James Walker" could have it. He had friends; he liked company. That brings up that picture of him, the time that I saw him last. The pathos of it! It comes before me often and often. At that very time, poor thing, I was girding up my conscience to make him move on again!

Hillyer's heart is better than mine, better than anybody's in the community, I suppose, for he is the one friend of the black sheep of the camp — Flint Buckner — and the only man Flint ever talks with or allows to talk with him. He says he knows Flint's history, and that it is trouble that has made him what he is, and so one ought to be as charitable toward him as one can. Now none but a pretty large heart could find space to accommodate a lodger like Flint Buckner, from all I hear about him outside. I think that this one detail will give you a better idea of Sammy's character than any labored-out description I could furnish you of him. In one of our talks he said something about like this: "Flint is a kinsman of mine, and he pours out all his troubles to me — empties his breast from time to time, or I reckon it would burst. There couldn't be any unhappier man, Archy Stillman; his life had been made up of misery of mind — he isn't near as old as he looks. He has lost the feel of reposefulness and peace — oh, years and years ago! He doesn't know what good luck is — never has had any; often says he wishes he was in the other hell, he is so tired of this one."

IV.

"NO REAL GENTLEMAN will tell the naked truth in the presence of ladies."

It was a crisp and spicy morning in early October. The lilacs and laburnums, lit with the glory-fires of autumn, hung burning and flashing in the upper air, a fairy bridge provided by kind Nature for the wingless wild things that have their homes in the tree-tops and would visit together; the larch and the pomegranate flung their purple and yellow flames in brilliant broad splashes along the slanting sweep of the woodland; the sensuous fragrance of innumerable deciduous flowers rose upon the swooning atmosphere; far in the empty sky a solitary oesophagus slept upon motionless wing; everywhere brooded stillness, serenity, and the peace of God.

October is the time — 1900; Hope Canyon is the place, a silver-mining camp away down in the Esmeralda region. It is a secluded spot, high and remote; recent as to discovery; thought by its occupants to be rich in metal — a year or two's prospecting will decide that matter one way or the other. For inhabitants, the camp has about two hundred miners, one white woman and child, several Chinese washermen, five squaws, and a dozen vagrant buck Indians in rabbit-skin robes, battered plug hats, and tin-can necklaces. There are no mills as yet; there is no church, no newspaper. The camp has existed but two years; it has made no big strike; the world is ignorant of its name and place.

On both sides of the canyon the mountains rise wall-like, three thousand feet, and the long spiral of straggling huts down in its narrow bottom gets a kiss from the sun only once a day, when he sails over at noon. The village is a couple of miles long; the cabins stand well apart from each other. The tavern is the only "frame" house — the only house, one might say. It occupies a central position, and is the evening resort of the population. They drink there, and play seven-up and dominoes; also billiards, for there is a table, crossed all over with torn places repaired with court-plaster; there are some cues, but no leathers; some chipped balls which clatter when they run, and do not slow up gradually, but stop suddenly and sit down; there is part of a cube of chalk, with a projecting jag of flint in it; and the man who can score six on a single break can set up the drinks at the bar's expense.

Flint Buckner's cabin was the last one of the village, going south; his silver-claim was at the other end of the village, northward, and a little beyond the last hut in that direction. He was a sour creature, unsociable, and had no companionships. People who had tried to get acquainted with him had regretted it and dropped him. His history was not known. Some believed that Sammy Hillyer knew it; others said no. If asked, Hillyer said no, he was not acquainted with it. Flint had a meek English youth of sixteen or seventeen with him, whom he treated roughly, both in public and in private, and of course this lad was applied to for information, but with no success. Fetlock Jones — the name of the youth — said that Flint picked him up on a prospecting tramp, and as he had neither home nor friends in America, he had found it wise to stay and take Buckner's hard usage for the sake of the salary, which was bacon and beans. Further than this he could offer no testimony.

Fetlock had been in this slavery for a month now, and under his meek exterior he was slowly consuming to a cinder with the insults and humiliations which his master had put upon him. For the meek suffer bitterly from these hurts; more bitterly, perhaps, than do the manlier sort, who can burst out and get relief with words or blows when the limit of endurance has been reached. Good-hearted people wanted to help Fetlock out of his trouble, and tried to get him to leave Buckner; but the boy showed fright at the thought, and said he "dasn't." Pat Riley urged him, and said,

"You leave the damned hunks and come with me; don't you be afraid. I'll take care of him."

The boy thanked him with tears in his eyes, but shuddered and said he "dasn't risk it"; he said Flint would catch him alone, some time, in the night, and then — "Oh, it makes me sick, Mr. Riley, to think of it."

Others said, "Run away from him; we'll stake you; skip out for the coast some night." But all these suggestions failed; he said Flint would hunt him down and fetch him back, just for meanness.

The people could not understand this. The boy's miseries went steadily on, week after week. It is quite likely that the people would have understood if they had known how he was employing his spare time. He slept in an out-cabin near Flint's; and there, nights, he nursed his bruises and his humiliations, and studied and studied over a single problem — how he could murder Flint Buckner and not be found out. It was the only joy he had in life; these hours were the only ones in the twenty-four which he looked forward to with eagerness and spent in happiness.

He thought of poison. No — that would not serve; the inquest would reveal where it was procured and who had procured it. He thought of a shot in the back in a lonely place when Flint would be homeward-bound at midnight — his unvarying hour for the trip. No — somebody might be near, and catch him. He thought of stabbing him in his sleep. No — he might strike an inefficient blow, and Flint would seize him. He examined a hundred different ways — none of them would answer; for in even the very obscurest and secretest of them there was always the fatal defect of a risk, a chance, a possibility that he might be found out. He would have none of that.

But he was patient, endlessly patient. There was no hurry, he said to himself. He would never leave Flint till he left him a corpse; there was no hurry — he would find the way. It was somewhere, and he would endure shame and pain and misery until he found it. Yes, somewhere there was a way which would leave not a trace, not even the faintest clue to the murderer — there was no hurry — he would find that way, and then — oh, then, it would just be good to be alive! Meantime he would diligently keep up his reputation for meekness; and also, as always theretofore, he would allow no one to hear him say a resentful or offensive thing about his oppressor.

Two days before the before-mentioned October morning Flint had bought some things, and he and Fetlock had brought them home to Flint's cabin: a fresh box of candles, which they put in the corner; a tin can of blasting-powder, which they placed upon the candle-box; a keg of blasting-powder, which they placed under Flint's bunk; a huge coil of fuse, which they hung on a peg. Fetlock reasoned that Flint's mining operations had outgrown the pick, and that blasting was about to begin now. He had seen blasting done, and he had a notion of the process, but he had never helped in it. His conjecture was right — blasting-time had come. In the morning the pair carried fuse, drills, and the powder-can to the shaft; it was now eight feet deep, and to get into it and out of it a short ladder was used. They descended, and by command Fetlock held the drill — without any instructions as to the right way to hold it — and Flint proceeded to strike. The sledge came down; the drill sprang out of Fetlock's hand, almost as a matter of course.

"You mangy son of a nigger, is that any way to hold a drill? Pick it up! Stand it up! There — hold fast. D — you! I'll teach you!"

At the end of an hour the drilling was finished.

"Now, then, charge it."

The boy started to pour in the powder.

"Idiot!"

A heavy bat on the jaw laid the lad out.

"Get up! You can't lie snivelling there. Now, then, stick in the fuse first. Now put in the powder. Hold on, hold on! Are you going to fill the hole all up? Of all the sap-headed milksops I — Put in some dirt! Put in some gravel! Tamp it down! Hold on, hold on! Oh, great Scott! Get out of the way!" He snatched the iron and tamped the charge himself, meantime cursing and blaspheming like a fiend. Then he fired the fuse, climbed out of the shaft, and ran fifty yards away, Fetlock following. They stood waiting a few minutes, then a great volume of smoke and rocks burst high into the air with a thunderous explosion; after a little there was a shower of descending stones; then all was serene again.

"I wish to God you'd been in it!" remarked the master.

They went down the shaft, cleaned it out, drilled another hole, and put in another charge.

"Look here! How much fuse are you proposing to waste? Don't you know how to time a fuse?"

"No, sir."

"You don't! Well, if you don't beat anything I ever saw!"

He climbed out of the shaft and spoke down,

"Well, idiot, are you going to be all day? Cut the fuse and light it!"

The trembling creature began,

"If you please, sir, I — "

"You talk back to me? Cut it and light it!"

The boy cut and lit.

"Ger-reat Scott! A one-minute fuse! I wish you were in — "

In his rage he snatched the ladder out of the shaft and ran. The boy was aghast.

"Oh, my God! Help. Help! Oh, save me!" he implored. "Oh, what can I do! What can I do!"

He backed against the wall as tightly as he could; the sputtering fuse frightened the voice out of him; his breath stood still; he stood gazing and impotent; in two seconds, three seconds, four he would be flying toward the sky torn to fragments. Then he had an inspiration. He sprang at the fuse, severed the inch of it that was left above ground, and was saved.

He sank down limp and half lifeless with fright, his strength all gone; but he muttered with a deep joy,

"He has learnt me! I knew there was a way, if I would wait."

After a matter of five minutes Buckner stole to the shaft, looking worried and uneasy, and peered down into it. He took in the situation; he saw what had happened. He lowered the ladder, and the boy dragged himself weakly up it. He was very white. His appearance added something to Buckner's uncomfortable state, and he said, with a show of regret and sympathy which sat upon him awkwardly from lack of practice:

"It was an accident, you know. Don't say anything about it to anybody; I was excited, and didn't notice what I was doing. You're not looking well; you've worked enough for to-day; go down to my cabin and eat what you want, and rest. It's just an accident, you know, on account of my being excited."

"It scared me," said the lad, as he started away; "but I learnt something, so I don't mind it."

"Damned easy to please!" muttered Buckner, following him with his eye. "I wonder if he'll tell? Mightn't he?... I wish it had killed him."

The boy took no advantage of his holiday in the matter of resting; he employed it in work, eager and feverish and happy work. A thick growth of chaparral extended down the mountainside clear to Flint's cabin; the most of Fetlock's labor was done in the dark intricacies of that stubborn growth; the rest of it was done in his own shanty. At last all was complete, and he said,

"If he's got any suspicions that I'm going to tell on him, he won't keep them long, to-morrow. He will see that I am the same milksop as I always was — all day and the next. And the day after tomorrow night there 'll be an end of him; nobody will ever guess who finished him up nor how it was done. He dropped me the idea his own self, and that's odd."

V

THE NEXT DAY CAME AND WENT.

It is now almost midnight, and in five minutes the new morning will begin. The scene is in the tavern billiard-room. Rough men in rough clothing, slouch-hats, breeches stuffed into boot-tops, some with vests, none with coats, are grouped about the boiler-iron stove, which has ruddy cheeks and is distributing a grateful warmth; the billiard-balls are clacking; there is no other sound — that is, within; the wind is fitfully moaning without. The men look bored; also expectant. A hulking broad-shouldered miner, of middle age, with grizzled whiskers, and an unfriendly eye set in an unsociable face, rises, slips a coil of fuse upon his arm, gathers up some other personal properties, and departs without word or greeting to anybody. It is Flint Buckner. As the door closes behind him a buzz of talk breaks out.

"The regularest man that ever was," said Jake Parker, the blacksmith; "you can tell when it's twelve just by him leaving, without looking at your Waterbury."

"And it's the only virtue he's got, as fur as I know," said Peter Hawes, miner.

"He's just a blight on this society," said Wells-Fargo's man, Ferguson. "If I was running this shop I'd make him say something, some time or other, or vamos the ranch." This with a suggestive glance at the barkeeper, who did not choose to see it, since the man under discussion was a good customer, and went home pretty well set up, every night, with refreshments furnished from the bar.

"Say," said Ham Sandwich, miner, "does any of you boys ever recollect of him asking you to take a drink?"

"Him? Flint Buckner? Oh, Laura!"

This sarcastic rejoinder came in a spontaneous general outburst in one form of words or another from the crowd. After a brief silence, Pat Riley, miner, said,

"He's the 15-puzzle, that cuss. And his boy's another one. I can't make them out."

"Nor anybody else," said Ham Sandwich; "and if they are 15-puzzles how are you going to rank up that other one? When it comes to A 1 right-down solid mysteriousness, he lays over both of them. Easy — don't he?"

"You bet!"

Everybody said it. Every man but one. He was the new-comer — Peterson. He ordered the drinks all round, and asked who No. 3 might be. All answered at once, "Archy Stillman!"

"Is he a mystery?" asked Peterson.

"Is he a mystery? Is Archy Stillman a mystery?" said Wells-Fargo's man, Ferguson. "Why, the fourth dimension's foolishness to him."

For Ferguson was learned.

Peterson wanted to hear all about him; everybody wanted to tell him; everybody began. But Billy Stevens, the barkeeper, called the house to order, and said one at a time was best. He distributed the drinks, and appointed Ferguson to lead. Ferguson said,

"Well, he's a boy. And that is just about all we know about him. You can pump him till you are tired; it ain't any use; you won't get anything. At least about his intentions, or line of business, or where he's from, and such things as that. And as for getting at the nature and get-up of his main big chief mystery, why, he'll just change the subject, that's all. You can guess till you're black in the face — it's your privilege — but suppose you do, where do you arrive at? Nowhere, as near as I can make out."

"What is his big chief one?"

"Sight, maybe. Hearing, maybe. Instinct, maybe. Magic, maybe. Take your choice — grownups, twenty-five, children and servants, half price. Now I'll tell you what he can do. You can start here, and just disappear; you can go and hide wherever you want to, I don't care where it is, nor how far — and he'll go straight and put his finger on you."

"You don't mean it!"

"I just do, though. Weather's nothing to him — elemental conditions is nothing to him — he don't even take notice of them."

"Oh, come! Dark? Rain? Snow? Hey?"

"It's all the same to him. He don't give a damn."

"Oh, say — including fog, per'aps?"

"Fog! he's got an eye 't can plunk through it like a bullet."

"Now, boys, honor bright, what's he giving me?"

"It's a fact!" they all shouted. "Go on, Wells-Fargo."

"Well, sir, you can leave him here, chatting with the boys, and you can slip out and go to any cabin in this camp and open a book — yes, sir, a dozen of them — and take the page in your memory, and he'll start out and go straight to that cabin and open every one of them books at the right page, and call it off, and never make a mistake."

"He must be the devil!"

"More than one has thought it. Now I'll tell you a perfectly wonderful thing that he done. The other night he — "

There was a sudden great murmur of sounds outside, the door flew open, and an excited crowd burst in, with the camp's one white woman in the lead and crying,

"My child! My child! She's lost and gone! For the love of God help me to find Archy Stillman; we've hunted everywhere!"

Said the barkeeper:

"Sit down, sit down, Mrs. Hogan, and don't worry. He asked for a bed three hours ago, tuckered out tramping the trails the way he's always doing, and went upstairs. Ham Sandwich, run up and roust him out; he's in No. 14."

The youth was soon downstairs and ready. He asked Mrs. Hogan for particulars.

"Bless you, dear, there ain't any; I wish there was. I put her to sleep at seven in the evening, and when I went in there an hour ago to go to bed myself, she was gone. I rushed for your cabin, dear, and you wasn't there, and I've hunted for you ever since, at every cabin down the gulch, and now

I've come up again, and I'm that distracted and scared and heart-broke; but, thanks to God, I've found you at last, dear heart, and you'll find my child. Come on! Come quick!"

"Move right along; I'm with you, madam. Go to your cabin first."

The whole company streamed out to join the hunt. All the southern half of the village was up, a hundred men strong, and waiting outside, a vague dark mass sprinkled with twinkling lanterns. The mass fell into columns by threes and fours to accommodate itself to the narrow road, and strode briskly along southward in the wake of the leaders. In a few minutes the Hogan cabin was reached.

"There's the bunk," said Mrs. Hogan; "there's where she was; it's where I laid her at seven o'clock; but where she is now, God only knows."

"Hand me a lantern," said Archy. He set it on the hard earth floor and knelt by it, pretending to examine the ground closely. "Here's her track," he said, touching the ground here and there and yonder with his finger. "Do you see?"

Several of the company dropped upon their knees and did their best to see. One or two thought they discerned something like a track; the others shook their heads and confessed that the smooth hard surface had no marks upon it which their eyes were sharp enough to discover. One said, "Maybe a child's foot could make a mark on it, but I don't see how."

Young Stillman stepped outside, held the light to the ground, turned leftward, and moved three steps, closely examining, then said, "I've got the direction — come along; take the lantern, somebody."

He strode off swiftly southward, the files following, swaying and bending in and out with the deep curves of the gorge. Thus a mile, and the mouth of the gorge was reached; before them stretched the sagebrush plain, dim, vast, and vague. Stillman called a halt, saying, "We mustn't start wrong, now; we must take the direction again."

He took a lantern and examined the ground for a matter of twenty yards; then said, "Come on; it's all right," and gave up the lantern. In and out among the sage-bushes he marched, a quarter of a mile, bearing gradually to the right; then took a new direction and made another great semicircle; then changed again and moved due west nearly half a mile — and stopped.

"She gave it up, here, poor little chap. Hold the lantern. You can see where she sat."

But this was in a slick alkali flat which was surfaced like steel, and no person in the party was quite hardy enough to claim an eyesight that could detect the track of a cushion on a veneer like that. The bereaved mother fell upon her knees and kissed the spot, lamenting.

"But where is she, then?" some one said. "She didn't stay here. We can see that much, anyway."

Stillman moved about in a circle around the place, with the lantern, pretending to hunt for tracks.

"Well!" he said presently, in an annoyed tone, "I don't understand it." He examined again. "No use. She was here — that's certain; she never walked away from here — and that's certain. It's a puzzle; I can't make it out."

The mother lost heart then.

"Oh, my God! Oh, blessed Virgin! Some flying beast has got her. I'll never see her again!"

"Ah, don't give up," said Archy. "We'll find her — don't give up."

"God bless you for the words, Archy Stillman!" and she seized his hand and kissed it fervently.

Peterson, the new-comer, whispered satirically in Ferguson's ear:

"Wonderful performance to find this place, wasn't it? Hardly worth while to come so far, though; any other supposititious place would have answered just as well — hey?"

Ferguson was not pleased with the innuendo. He said, with some warmth,

"Do you mean to insinuate that the child hasn't been here? I tell you the child has been here! Now if you want to get yourself into as tidy a little fuss as — "

"All right!" sang out Stillman. "Come, everybody, and look at this! It was right under our noses all the time, and we didn't see it."

There was a general plunge for the ground at the place where the child was alleged to have rested, and many eyes tried hard and hopefully to see the thing that Archy's finger was resting upon. There was a pause, then a several-barrelled sigh of disappointment. Pat Riley and Ham Sandwich said, in the one breath,

"What is it, Archy? There's nothing here."

"Nothing? Do you call that nothing?" and he swiftly traced upon the ground a form with his finger. "There — don't you recognize it now? It's Injun Billy's track. He's got the child."

"God be praised!" from the mother.

"Take away the lantern. I've got the direction. Follow!"

He started on a run, racing in and out among the sage-bushes a matter of three hundred yards, and disappeared over a sand-wave; the others struggled after him, caught him up, and found him waiting. Ten steps away was a little wickieup, a dim and formless shelter of rags and old horse-blankets, a dull light showing through its chinks.

"You lead, Mrs. Hogan," said the lad. "It's your privilege to be first."

All followed the sprint she made for the wickieup, and saw, with her, the picture its interior afforded. Injun Billy was sitting on the ground; the child was asleep beside him. The mother hugged it with a wild embrace, which included Archy Stillman, the grateful tears running down her face, and in a choked and broken voice she poured out a golden stream of that wealth of worshiping endearments which has its home in full richness nowhere but in the Irish heart.

"I find her bymeby it is ten o'clock," Billy explained. "She 'sleep out yonder, ve'y tired — face wet, been cryin', 'spose; fetch her home, feed her, she heap much hungry — go 'sleep 'gin."

In her limitless gratitude the happy mother waived rank and hugged him too, calling him "the angel of God in disguise." And he probably was in disguise if he was that kind of an official. He was dressed for the character.

At half past one in the morning the procession burst into the village singing, "When Johnny Comes Marching Home," waving its lanterns, and swallowing the drinks that were brought out all along its course. It concentrated at the tavern, and made a night of what was left of the morning.

PART II

I

THE NEXT AFTERNOON the village was electrified with an immense sensation. A grave and dignified foreigner of distinguished bearing and appearance had arrived at the tavern, and entered this formidable name upon the register:

SHERLOCK HOLMES.

The news buzzed from cabin to cabin, from claim to claim; tools were dropped, and the town swarmed toward the center of interest. A man passing out at the northern end of the village shouted it to Pat Riley, whose claim was the next one to Flint Buckner's. At that time Fetlock Jones seemed to turn sick. He muttered to himself,

"Uncle Sherlock! The mean luck of it! — That he should come just when...."

He dropped into a reverie, and presently said to himself: "But what's the use of being afraid of him? Anybody that knows him the way I do knows he can't detect a crime except where he plans it all out beforehand and arranges the clues and hires some fellow to commit it according to instructions.... Now there ain't going to be any clues this time — so, what show has he got? None at all. No, sir; everything's ready. If I was to risk putting it off.... No, I won't run any risk like that. Flint Buckner goes out of this world to-night, for sure." Then another trouble presented itself. "Uncle Sherlock'll be wanting to talk home matters with me this evening, and how am I going to get rid of him? For I've got to be at my cabin a minute or two about eight o'clock." This was an awkward matter, and cost him much thought. But he found a way to beat the difficulty. "We'll go for a walk, and I'll leave him in the road a minute, so that he won't see what it is I do: the best way to throw a detective off the track, anyway, is to have

him along when you are preparing the thing. Yes, that's the safest — I'll take him with me."

Meantime the road in front of the tavern was blocked with villagers waiting and hoping for a glimpse of the great man. But he kept his room, and did not appear. None but Ferguson, Jake Parker the blacksmith, and Ham Sandwich had any luck. These enthusiastic admirers of the great scientific detective hired the tavern's detained-baggage lockup, which looked into the detective's room across a little alleyway ten or twelve feet wide, ambushed themselves in it, and cut some peep-holes in the window-blind. Mr. Holmes' blinds were down; but by-and-by he raised them. It gave the spies a hair-lifting but pleasurable thrill to find themselves face to face with the Extraordinary Man who had filled the world with the fame of his more than human ingenuities. There he sat — not a myth, not a shadow, but real, alive, compact of substance, and almost within touching distance with the hand.

"Look at that head!" said Ferguson, in an awed voice. "By gracious! that's a head!"

"You bet!" said the blacksmith, with deep reverence. "Look at his nose! Look at his eyes! Intellect? Just a battery of it!"

"And that paleness," said Ham Sandwich. "Comes from thought — that's what it comes from. Hell! Duffers like us don't know what real thought is."

"No more we don't," said Ferguson. "What we take for thinking is just blubber-and-slush."

"Right you are, Wells-Fargo. And look at that frown — that's deep thinking — away down, down, forty fathom into the bowels of things. He's on the track of something."

"Well, he is, and don't you forget it. Say — look at that awful gravity — look at that pallid solemness — there ain't any corpse can lay over it."

"No, sir, not for dollars! And it's his'n by hereditary rights, too; he's been dead four times a'ready, and there's history for it. Three times natural, once by accident. I've heard say he smells damp and cold, like a grave. And he — "

"'Sh! Watch him! There — he's got his thumb on the bump on the near corner of his forehead, and his forefinger on the off one. His think-works is just a-grinding now, you bet your other shirt."

"That's so. And now he's gazing up toward heaven and stroking his mustache slow, and — "

"Now he has rose up standing, and is putting his clues together on his left fingers with his right finger. See? He touches the forefinger — now middle finger — now ring-finger — "

"Stuck!"

"Look at him scowl! He can't seem to make out that clue. So he — "

"See him smile! — like a tiger — and tally off the other fingers like nothing! He's got it, boys; he's got it sure!"

"Well, I should say! I'd hate to be in that man's place that he's after."

Mr. Holmes drew a table to the window, sat down with his back to the spies, and proceeded to write. The spies withdrew their eyes from the peep-holes, lit their pipes, and settled themselves for a comfortable smoke and talk. Ferguson said, with conviction,

"Boys, it's no use talking, he's a wonder! He's got the signs of it all over him."

"You hain't ever said a truer word than that, Wells-Fargo," said Jake Parker. "Say, wouldn't it 'a' been nuts if he'd a-been here last night?"

"Oh, by George, but wouldn't it!" said Ferguson. "Then we'd have seen scientific work. Intellect — just pure intellect — away up on the upper levels, dontchuknow. Archy is all right, and it don't become anybody to belittle him, I can tell you. But his gift is only just eyesight, sharp as an owl's, as near as I can make it out just a grand natural animal talent, no more, no less, and prime as far as it goes, but no intellect in it, and for awfulness and marvelousness no more to be compared to what this man does than — than — Why, let me tell you what he'd have done. He'd have stepped over to Hogan's and glanced — just glanced, that's all — at the premises, and that's enough. See everything? Yes, sir, to the last little detail, and he'll know more about that place than the

Hogans would know in seven years. Next, he would sit down on the bunk, just as ca'm, and say to Mrs. Hogan — Say, Ham, consider that you are Mrs. Hogan. I'll ask the questions; you answer them."

"All right; go on."

"'Madam, if you please — attention — do not let your mind wander. Now, then — sex of the child?'

"'Female, your Honor.'

"'Um — female. Very good, very good. Age?'

"'Turned six, your Honor.'

"'Um — young, weak — two miles. Weariness will overtake it then. It will sink down and sleep. We shall find it two miles away, or less. Teeth?'

"'Five, your Honor, and one a-coming.'

"'Very good, very good, very good, indeed.' You see, boys, he knows a clue when he sees it, when it wouldn't mean a dern thing to anybody else. 'Stockings, madam? Shoes?'

"'Yes, your Honor — both.'

"'Yarn, perhaps? Morocco?'

"'Yarn, your Honor. And kip.'

"'Um — kip. This complicates the matter. However, let it go — we shall manage. Religion?'

"'Catholic, your Honor.'

"'Very good. Snip me a bit from the bed blanket, please. Ah, thanks. Part wool — foreign make. Very well. A snip from some garment of the child's, please. Thanks. Cotton. Shows wear. An excellent clue, excellent. Pass me a pallet of the floor dirt, if you'll be so kind. Thanks, many thanks. Ah, admirable, admirable! Now we know where we are, I think.' You see, boys, he's got all the clues he wants now; he don't need anything more. Now, then, what does this Extraordinary Man do? He lays those snips and that dirt out on the table and leans over them on his elbows, and puts them together side by side and studies them — mumbles to himself, 'Female'; changes them around —

mumbles, 'Six years old'; changes them this way and that — again mumbles: 'Five teeth — one a-coming — Catholic — yarn — cotton — kip — damn that kip.' Then he straightens up and gazes toward heaven, and plows his hands through his hair — plows and plows, muttering, 'Damn that kip!' Then he stands up and frowns, and begins to tally off his clues on his fingers — and gets stuck at the ring-finger. But only just a minute — then his face glares all up in a smile like a house afire, and he straightens up stately and majestic, and says to the crowd, 'Take a lantern, a couple of you, and go down to Injun Billy's and fetch the child — the rest of you go 'long home to bed; good-night, madam; good-night, gents.' And he bows like the Matterhorn, and pulls out for the tavern. That's his style, and the Only — scientific, intellectual — all over in fifteen minutes — no poking around all over the sage-brush range an hour and a half in a mass-meeting crowd for him, boys — you hear me!"

"By Jackson, it's grand!" said Ham Sandwich. "Wells-Fargo, you've got him down to a dot. He ain't painted up any exacter to the life in the books. By George, I can just see him — can't you, boys?"

"You bet you! It's just a photograft, that's what it is."

Ferguson was profoundly pleased with his success, and grateful. He sat silently enjoying his happiness a little while, then he murmured, with a deep awe in his voice,

"I wonder if God made him?"

There was no response for a moment; then Ham Sandwich said, reverently, "Not all at one time, I reckon."

II

AT EIGHT O'CLOCK THAT EVENING two persons were groping their way past Flint Buckner's cabin in the frosty gloom. They were Sherlock Holmes and his nephew.

"Stop here in the road a moment, uncle," said Fetlock, "while I run to my cabin; I won't be gone a minute."

He asked for something — the uncle furnished it — then he disappeared in the darkness, but soon returned, and the talking-walk was resumed. By nine o'clock they had wandered back to the tavern. They worked their way through the billiard-room, where a crowd had gathered in the hope of getting a glimpse of the Extraordinary Man. A royal cheer was raised. Mr. Holmes acknowledged the compliment with a series of courtly bows, and as he was passing out his nephew said to the assemblage,

"Uncle Sherlock's got some work to do, gentlemen, that'll keep him till twelve or one; but he'll be down again then, or earlier if he can, and hopes some of you'll be left to take a drink with him."

"By George, he's just a duke, boys! Three cheers for Sherlock Holmes, the greatest man that ever lived!" shouted Ferguson. "Hip, hip, hip — "

"Hurrah! Hurrah! Hurrah! Tiger!"

The uproar shook the building, so hearty was the feeling the boys put into their welcome. Upstairs the uncle reproached the nephew gently, saying,

"What did you get me into that engagement for?"

"I reckon you don't want to be unpopular, do you, uncle? Well, then, don't you put on any exclusiveness in a mining-camp, that's all. The boys admire you; but if you was to leave without taking a drink with them, they'd set you down for a snob. And, besides, you said you had home talk enough in stock to keep us up and at it half the night."

The boy was right, and wise — the uncle acknowledged it. The boy was wise in another detail which he did not mention — except to himself: "Uncle and the others will come handy — in the way of nailing an alibi where it can't be budged."

He and his uncle talked diligently about three hours. Then, about midnight, Fetlock stepped down-stairs and took a position in the dark a dozen steps from the tavern, and waited. Five minutes later Flint Buckner came rocking out of the billiard-room and almost brushed him as he passed.

"I've got him!" muttered the boy. He continued to himself, looking after the shadowy form: "Good-by — good-by for good, Flint Buckner; you called my mother a — well, never mind what; it's all right, now; you're taking your last walk, friend."

He went musing back into the tavern. "From now till one is an hour. We'll spend it with the boys; it's good for the alibi."

He brought Sherlock Holmes to the billiard-room, which was jammed with eager and admiring miners; the guest called the drinks, and the fun began. Everybody was happy; everybody was complimentary; the ice was soon broken; songs, anecdotes, and more drinks followed, and the pregnant minutes flew. At six minutes to one, when the jollity was at its highest —

BOOM!

There was silence instantly. The deep sound came rolling and rumbling from peak to peak up the gorge, then died down, and ceased. The spell broke, then, and the men made a rush for the door, saying,

"Something's blown up!"

Outside, a voice in the darkness said, "It's away down the gorge; I saw the flash."

The crowd poured down the canyon — Holmes, Fetlock, Archy Stillman, everybody. They made the mile in a few minutes. By the light of a lantern they found the smooth and solid dirt floor of Flint Buckner's cabin; of the cabin itself not a vestige remained, not a rag nor a splinter. Nor any sign of Flint. Search-parties sought here and there and yonder, and presently a cry went up.

"Here he is!"

It was true. Fifty yards down the gulch they had found him — that is, they had found a crushed and lifeless mass which represented him. Fetlock Jones hurried thither with the others and looked.

The inquest was a fifteen-minute affair. Ham Sandwich, foreman of the jury, handed up the verdict, which was phrased with a certain unstudied literary grace, and closed with this finding, to wit: that "deceased came to his death by his own act or some other person or persons unknown to this jury not leaving any family or similar effects behind but his cabin which was blown away and God have mercy on his soul amen."

Then the impatient jury rejoined the main crowd, for the storm-centre of interest was there — Sherlock Holmes. The miners stood silent and reverent in a half-circle, inclosing a large vacant space which included the front exposure of the site of the late premises. In this considerable space the Extraordinary Man was moving about, attended by his nephew with a lantern. With a tape he took measurements of the cabin site, of the distance from the wall of chaparral to the road, of the height of the chaparral bushes; also various other measurements. He gathered a rag here, a splinter there, and a pinch of earth yonder, inspected them profoundly, and preserved them. He took the "lay" of the place with a pocket-compass, allowing two seconds for magnetic variation. He took the time (Pacific) by his watch, correcting it for local time. He paced off the distance from the cabin site to the corpse, and corrected that for tidal differentiation. He took the altitude with a pocket-aneroid, and the temperature with a pocket-thermometer. Finally he said, with a stately bow:

"It is finished. Shall we return, gentlemen?"

He took up the line of march for the tavern, and the crowd fell into his wake, earnestly discussing and admiring the Extraordinary Man, and interlarding guesses as to the origin of the tragedy and who the author of it might he.

"My, but it's grand luck having him here — hey, boys?" said Ferguson.

"It's the biggest thing of the century," said Ham Sandwich. "It'll go all over the world; you mark my words."

"You bet!" said Jake Parker, the blacksmith. "It'll boom this camp. Ain't it so, Wells-Fargo?"

"Well, as you want my opinion — if it's any sign of how I think about it, I can tell you this: yesterday I was holding the Straight Flush claim at two dollars a foot; I'd like to see the man that can get it at sixteen today."

"Right you are, Wells-Fargo! It's the grandest luck a new camp ever struck. Say, did you see him collar them little rags and dirt and things? What an eye! He just can't overlook a clue — 'tain't in him."

"That's so. And they wouldn't mean a thing to anybody else; but to him, why, they're just a book — large print at that."

"Sure's you're born! Them odds and ends have got their little old secret, and they think there ain't anybody can pull it; but, land! When he sets his grip there they've got to squeal, and don't you forget it."

"Boys, I ain't sorry, now, that he wasn't here to roust out the child; this is a bigger thing, by a long sight. Yes, sir, and more tangled up and scientific and intellectual."

"I reckon we're all of us glad it's turned out this way. Glad? 'George! It ain't any name for it. Dontchuknow, Archy could've learnt something if he'd had the nous to stand by and take notice of how that man works the system. But no; he went poking up into the chaparral and just missed the whole thing."

"It's true as gospel; I seen it myself. Well, Archy's young. He'll know better one of these days."

"Say, boys, who do you reckon done it?"

That was a difficult question, and brought out a world of unsatisfying conjecture. Various men were mentioned as possibilities, but one by one they were discarded as not being eligible. No one but young Hillyer had been intimate with Flint Buckner; no one had really had a quarrel with him; he had affronted every man who had tried to make up to him, although not quite offensively enough to require bloodshed. There was one name that was upon every tongue from the start, but it was the last to get utterance — Fetlock Jones'. It was Pat Riley that mentioned it.

"Oh, well," the boys said, "of course we've all thought of him, because he had a million rights to kill Flint Buckner, and it was just his plain duty to do it. But all the same there's two things we can't get around, for one thing, he hasn't got the sand; and for another, he wasn't anywhere near the place when it happened."

"I know it," said Pat. "He was there in the billiard-room with us when it happened."

"Yes, and was there all the time for an hour before it happened."

"It's so. And lucky for him, too. He'd have been suspected in a minute if it hadn't been for that."

III

THE TAVERN DINING ROOM had been cleared of all its furniture save one six-foot pine table and a chair. This table was against one end of the room; the chair was on it; Sherlock Holmes, stately, imposing, impressive, sat in the chair. The public stood. The room was full. The tobacco-smoke was dense, the stillness profound.

The Extraordinary Man raised his hand to command additional silence; held it in the air a few moments; then, in brief, crisp terms he put forward question after question, and noted the answers with "Um-ums," nods of the head, and so on. By this process he learned all about Flint Buckner, his character, conduct, and habits, that the people were able to tell him. It thus transpired that the Extraordinary Man's nephew was the only person in the camp who had a killing-grudge against Flint Buckner. Mr. Holmes smiled compassionately upon the witness, and asked, languidly —

"Do any of you gentlemen chance to know where the lad Fetlock Jones was at the time of the explosion?"

A thunderous response followed —

"In the billiard-room of this house!"

"Ah. And had he just come in?"

"Been there all of an hour!"

"Ah. It is about — about — well, about how far might it be to the scene of the explosions."

"All of a mile!"

"Ah. It isn't much of an alibi, 'tis true, but — "

A storm-burst of laughter, mingled with shouts of "By jiminy, but he's chain-lightning!" and "Ain't you sorry you spoke, Sandy?" shut off the rest of the sentence, and the crushed witness drooped his blushing face in pathetic shame. The inquisitor resumed:

"The lad Jones's somewhat distant connection with the case" (laughter) "having been disposed of, let us now call the eye-witnesses of the tragedy, and listen to what they have to say."

He got out his fragmentary clues and arranged them on a sheet of cardboard on his knee. The house held its breath and watched.

"We have the longitude and the latitude, corrected for magnetic variation, and this gives us the exact location of the tragedy. We have the altitude, the temperature, and the degree of humidity prevailing — inestimably valuable, since they enable us to estimate with precision the degree of influence which they would exercise upon the mood and disposition of the assassin at that time of the night."

(Buzz of admiration; muttered remark, "By George, but he's deep!") He fingered his clues. "And now let us ask these mute witnesses to speak to us.

"Here we have an empty linen shot-bag. What is its message? This: that robbery was the motive, not revenge. What is its further message? This: that the assassin was of inferior intelligence — shall we say light-witted, or perhaps approaching that? How do we know this? Because a person of sound intelligence would not have proposed to rob the man Buckner, who never had much money with him. But the assassin might have been a stranger? Let the bag speak again. I take from it this article. It is a bit of silver-bearing quartz. It is peculiar. Examine it, please — you — and you — and you. Now pass it back, please. There is but one lode on this coast which produces just that character and color of quartz; and that is a lode which crops out for nearly two miles on a stretch, and in my opinion is destined, at no distant day, to confer upon its locality a globe-girdling celebrity, and upon its two hundred owners riches beyond the dreams of avarice. Name that lode, please."

"The Consolidated Christian Science and Mary Ann!" was the prompt response.

A wild crash of hurrahs followed, and every man reached for his neighbor's hand and wrung it, with tears in his eyes; and Wells-Fargo Ferguson shouted, "The Straight Flush is on the lode, and up she goes to a hunched and fifty a foot — you hear me!"

When quiet fell, Mr. Holmes resumed:

"We perceive, then, that three facts are established, to wit: the assassin was approximately light-witted; he was not a stranger; his motive was robbery, not revenge. Let us proceed. I hold in my hand a small fragment of fuse, with the recent smell of fire upon it. What is its testimony? Taken with the corroborative evidence of the quartz, it reveals to us that the assassin was a miner. What does it tell us further? This, gentlemen: that the assassination was consummated by means of an explosive. What else does it say? This: that the explosive was located against the side of the cabin nearest the road — the front side — for within six feet of that spot I found it.

"I hold in my fingers a burnt Swedish match — the kind one rubs on a safety-box. I found it in the road, six hundred and twenty-two feet from the abolished cabin. What does it say? This: that the train was fired from that point. What further does it tell us? This: that the assassin was left-handed. How do I know this? I should not be able to explain to you, gentlemen, how I know it, the signs being so subtle that only long experience and deep study can enable one to detect them. But the signs are here, and they are reinforced by a fact which you must have often noticed in the great detective narratives — that all assassins are left-handed."

"By Jackson, that's so!" said Ham Sandwich, bringing his great hand down with a resounding slap upon his thigh. "Blamed if I ever thought of it before."

"Nor I!" "Nor I!" cried several. "Oh, there can't anything escape him — look at his eye!"

"Gentlemen, distant as the murderer was from his doomed victim, he did not wholly escape injury. This fragment of wood which I now exhibit to you struck him. It drew blood. Wherever he is, he bears the telltale mark. I picked it up where he stood when he fired the fatal train." He looked out over the house from his high perch, and his countenance began to darken; he slowly raised his hand, and pointed —

"There stands the assassin!"

For a moment the house was paralyzed with amazement; then twenty voices burst out with:

"Sammy Hillyer? Oh, hell, no! Him? It's pure foolishness!"

"Take care, gentlemen — be not hasty. Observe — he has the blood-mark on his brow."

Hillyer turned white with fright. He was near to crying. He turned this way and that, appealing to every face for help and sympathy; and held out his supplicating hands toward Holmes and began to plead,

"Don't, oh, don't! I never did it; I give my word I never did it. The way I got this hurt on my forehead was — "

"Arrest him, constable!" cried Holmes. "I will swear out the warrant."

The constable moved reluctantly forward — hesitated — stopped.

Hillyer broke out with another appeal. "Oh, Archy, don't let them do it; it would kill mother! You know how I got the hurt. Tell them, and save me, Archy; save me!"

Stillman worked his way to the front, and said,

"Yes, I'll save you. Don't be afraid." Then he said to the house, "Never mind how he got the hurt; it hasn't anything to do with this case, and isn't of any consequence."

"God bless you, Archy, for a true friend!"

"Hurrah for Archy! Go in, boy, and play 'em a knock-down flush to their two pair 'n' a jack!" shouted the house, pride in their home talent and a patriotic sentiment of loyalty to it rising suddenly in the public heart and changing the whole attitude of the situation.

Young Stillman waited for the noise to cease; then he said,

"I will ask Tom Jeffries to stand by that door yonder, and Constable Harris to stand by the other one here, and not let anybody leave the room."

"Said and done. Go on, old man!"

"The criminal is present, I believe. I will show him to you before long, in case I am right in my guess. Now I will tell you all about the tragedy, from start to finish. The motive wasn't robbery; it was revenge. The murderer wasn't light-witted. He didn't stand six hundred and twenty-two feet away. He didn't get hit with a piece of wood. He didn't place the explosive against the cabin. He didn't bring a shot-bag with him, and he wasn't left-handed. With the exception of these errors, the distinguished guest's statement of the case is substantially correct."

A comfortable laugh rippled over the house; friend nodded to friend, as much as to say, "That's the word, with the bark on it. Good lad, good boy. He ain't lowering his flag any!"

The guest's serenity was not disturbed. Stillman resumed:

"I also have some witnesses; and I will presently tell you where you can find some more." He held up a piece of coarse wire; the crowd craned their necks to see. "It has a smooth coating of melted tallow on it. And here is a candle which is burned half-way down. The remaining half of it has marks cut upon it an inch apart. Soon I will tell you where I found these things. I will now put aside reasonings, guesses, the impressive hitchings of odds and ends of clues together, and the other showy theatricals of the detective trade, and tell you in a plain, straightforward way just how this dismal thing happened."

He paused a moment, for effect — to allow silence and suspense to intensify and concentrate the house's interest; then he went on:

"The assassin studied out his plan with a good deal of pains. It was a good plan, very ingenious, and showed an intelligent mind, not a feeble one. It was a plan which was well calculated to ward off all suspicion from its inventor. In the first place, he marked a candle into spaces an inch apart, and lit it and timed it. He found it took three hours to burn four inches of it. I tried it myself for half an hour, awhile ago, up-stairs here, while the inquiry into Flint Buckner's character and ways was being conducted in this room, and I arrived in that way at the rate of a candle's consumption when sheltered from the wind. Having proved his trial candle's rate, he blew it out — I have already shown it to you — and put his inch-marks on a fresh one.

"He put the fresh one into a tin candlestick. Then at the five-hour mark he bored a hole through the candle with a red-hot wire. I have already shown you the wire, with a smooth coat of tallow on it — tallow that had been melted and had cooled.

"With labor — very hard labor, I should say — he struggled up through the stiff chaparral that clothes the steep hillside back of Flint Buckner's place, tugging an empty flour-barrel with him. He placed it in that absolutely secure hiding-place, and in the bottom of it he set the candlestick. Then he measured off about thirty-five feet of fuse — the barrel's distance from the back of the cabin. He bored a hole in the side of the barrel — here is the large gimlet he did it with. He went on and finished his work; and when it was done, one end of the fuse was in Buckner's cabin, and the other end, with a notch chipped in it to expose the powder, was in the hole in the candle — timed to blow the place up at one o'clock this morning, provided the candle was lit about eight o'clock yesterday evening — which I am betting it was — and provided there was an explosive in the cabin and connected with that end of the fuse — which I am also betting there was, though I can't prove it. Boys, the barrel is there in the chaparral, the candle's remains are in it in the tin stick; the burnt-out fuse is in the gimlet-hole, the other end is down the hill where the late cabin stood. I saw them all an hour or two ago, when the Professor here was measuring off unimplicated vacancies and collecting relics that hadn't anything to do with the case."

He paused. The house drew a long, deep breath, shook its strained cords and muscles free and burst into cheers. "Dang him!" said Ham Sandwich, "that's why he was snooping around in the chaparral, instead of picking up points out of the P'fessor's game. Looky here — he ain't no fool, boys."

"No, sir! Why, great Scott — "

But Stillman was resuming:

"While we were out yonder an hour or two ago, the owner of the gimlet and the trial-candle took them from a place where he had concealed them — it was not a good place — and carried them to what he probably thought was a better one, two hundred yards up in the pine woods, and hid them there, covering them over with pine needles. It was there that I found them. The gimlet exactly fits the hole in the barrel. And now — "

The Extraordinary Man interrupted him. He said, sarcastically,

"We have had a very pretty fairy tale, gentlemen — very pretty indeed. Now I would like to ask this young man a question or two."

Some of the boys winced, and Ferguson said,

"I'm afraid Archy's going to catch it now."

The others lost their smiles and sobered down. Mr. Holmes said,

"Let us proceed to examine into this fairy-tale in a consecutive and orderly way — by geometrical progression, so to speak — linking detail to detail in a steadily advancing and remorselessly consistent and unassailable march upon this tinsel toy-fortress of error, the dream fabric of a callow-imagination. To begin with, young sir, I desire to ask you but three questions at present — at present. Did I understand you to say it was your opinion that the supposititious candle was lighted at about eight o'clock yesterday evening?"

"Yes, sir — about eight."

"Could you say exactly eight?"

"Well, no, I couldn't be that exact."

"Um. If a person had been passing along there just about that time, he would have been almost sure to encounter that assassin, do you think?"

"Yes, I should think so."

"Thank you, that is all. For the present. I say, all for the present."

"Dern him, he's laying for Archy," said Ferguson.

"It's so," said Ham Sandwich. "I don't like the look of it."

Stillman said, glancing at the guest, "I was along there myself at half past eight — no, about nine."

"Indeed? This is interesting — this is very interesting. Perhaps you encountered the assassin?"

"No, I encountered no one."

"Ah. Then — if you will excuse the remark — I do not quite see the relevancy of the information."

"It has none. At present. I say it has none — at present."

He paused. Presently he resumed: "I did not encounter the assassin, but I am on his track, I am sure, for I believe he is in this room. I will ask you all to pass one by one in front of me — here, where there is a good light — so that I can see your feet."

A buzz of excitement swept the place, and the march began, the guest looking on with an iron attempt at gravity which was not an unqualified success. Stillman stooped, shaded his eyes with his hand, and gazed down intently at each pair of feet as it passed. Fifty men tramped monotonously by — with no result. Sixty. Seventy. The thing was beginning to look absurd. The guest remarked, with suave irony,

"Assassins appear to be scarce this evening."

The house saw the humor if it, and refreshed itself with a cordial laugh. Ten or twelve more candidates tramped by — no, danced by, with airy and ridiculous capers which convulsed the spectators — then suddenly Stillman put out his hand and said,

"This is the assassin!"

"Fetlock Jones, by the great Sanhedrim!" roared the crowd; and at once let fly a pyrotechnic explosion and dazzle and confusion of stirring remarks inspired by the situation.

At the height of the turmoil the guest stretched out his hand, commanding peace. The authority of a great name and a great personality laid its mysterious compulsion upon the house, and it obeyed. Out of the panting calm which succeeded, the guest spoke, saying, with dignity and feeling,

"This is serious. It strikes at an innocent life. Innocent beyond suspicion! Innocent beyond peradventure! Hear me prove it; observe how simple a fact can brush out of existence this witless lie. Listen. My friends, that lad was never out of my sight yesterday evening at any time!"

It made a deep impression. Men turned their eyes upon Stillman with grave inquiry in them. His face brightened, and he said,

"I knew there was another one!" He stepped briskly to the table and glanced at the guest's feet, then up at his face, and said: "You were with him! You were not fifty steps from him when he lit the candle that by-and-by fired the powder!" (Sensation.) "And what is more, you furnished the matches yourself!"

Plainly the guest seemed hit; it looked so to the public. He opened his mouth to speak; the words did not come freely.

"This — er — this is insanity — this — "

Stillman pressed his evident advantage home. He held up a charred match.

"Here is one of them. I found it in the barrel — and there's another one there."

The guest found his voice at once.

"Yes — and put them there yourself!"

It was recognized a good shot. Stillman retorted.

"It is wax — a breed unknown to this camp. I am ready to be searched for the box. Are you?"

The guest was staggered this time — the dullest eye could see it. He fumbled with his hands; once or twice his lips moved, but the words did not come. The house waited and watched, in tense suspense, the stillness adding effect to the situation. Presently Stillman said, gently,

"We are waiting for your decision."

There was silence again during several moments; then the guest answered, in a low voice,

"I refuse to be searched."

There was no noisy demonstration, but all about the house one voice after another muttered,

"That settles it! He's Archy's meat."

What to do now? Nobody seemed to know. It was an embarrassing situation for the moment — merely, of course, because matters had taken such a sudden and unexpected turn that these unpractised minds were not prepared for it, and had come to a standstill, like a stopped clock, under the shock. But after a little the machinery began to work again, tentatively, and by twos and threes the men put their heads together and privately buzzed over this and that and the other proposition. One of these propositions met with much favor; it was, to confer upon the assassin a vote of thanks for removing Flint Buckner, and let him go. But the cooler heads opposed it, pointing out that addled brains in the Eastern states would pronounce it a scandal, and make no end of foolish noise about it. Finally the cool heads got the upper hand, and obtained general consent to a proposition of their own; their leader then called the house to order and stated it — to this effect: that Fetlock Jones be jailed and put upon trial.

The motion was carried. Apparently there was nothing further to do now, and the people were glad, for, privately, they were impatient to get out and rush to the scene of the tragedy, and see whether that barrel and the other things were really there or not.

But no — the break-up got a check. The surprises were not over yet. For a while Fetlock Jones had been silently sobbing, unnoticed in the absorbing excitements which had been following one another so persistently for some time; but when his arrest and trial were decreed, he broke out despairingly, and said,

"No! it's no use. I don't want any jail, I don't want any trial; I've had all the hard luck I want, and all the miseries. Hang me now, and let me out! It would all come out, anyway — there couldn't anything save me. He has told it all, just as if he'd been with me and seen it — I don't know how he found out; and you'll find the barrel and things, and then I wouldn't have any chance any more. I killed him; and you'd have done it too, if he'd treated you like a dog, and you only a boy, and weak and poor, and not a friend to help you."

"And served him damned well right!" broke in Ham Sandwich. "Looky here, boys — "

From the constable: "Order! Order, gentlemen!"

A voice: "Did your uncle know what you was up to?"

"No, he didn't."

"Did he give you the matches, sure enough?"

"Yes, he did; but he didn't know what I wanted them for."

"When you was out on such a business as that, how did you venture to risk having him along — and him a detective? How's that?"

The boy hesitated, fumbled with his buttons in an embarrassed way, then said, shyly,

"I know about detectives, on account of having them in the family; and if you don't want them to find out about a thing, it's best to have them around when you do it."

The cyclone of laughter which greeted this naïve discharge of wisdom did not modify the poor little waif's embarrassment in any large degree.

IV

FROM A LETTER TO MRS. STILLMAN, dated merely "Tuesday."

Fetlock Jones was put under lock and key in an unoccupied log cabin, and left there to await his trial. Constable Harris provided him with a couple of days' rations, instructed him to keep a good guard over himself, and promised to look in on him as soon as further supplies should be due.

Next morning a score of us went with Hillyer, out of friendship, and helped him bury his late relative, the unlamented Buckner, and I acted as first assistant pall-bearer, Hillyer acting as chief. Just as we had finished our labors a ragged and melancholy stranger, carrying an old hand-bag, limped by with his head down, and I caught the scent I had chased around the globe! It was the odor of Paradise to my perishing hope!

In a moment I was at his side and had laid a gentle hand upon his shoulder. He slumped to the ground as if a stroke of lightning had withered him in his tracks; and as the boys came running he struggled to his knees and put up his pleading hands to me, and out of his chattering jaws he begged me to persecute him no more, and said,

"You have hunted me around the world, Sherlock Holmes, yet God is my witness I have never done any man harm!"

A glance at his wild eyes showed us that he was insane. That was my work, mother! The tidings of your death can some day repeat the misery I felt in that moment, but nothing else can ever do it. The boys lifted him up, and gathered about him, and were full of pity of him, and said the gentlest and touchingest things to him, and said cheer up and don't be troubled, he was among friends now, and they would take care of him, and protect him, and hang any man that laid a hand on him. They are just like so many mothers, the rough mining-camp boys are, when you wake up the south side of their hearts; yes, and just like so many reckless and unreasoning children when you wake up the opposite of that muscle. They did everything they could think of to comfort him, but nothing succeeded until Wells-Fargo Ferguson, who is a clever strategist, said,

"If it's only Sherlock Holmes that's troubling you, you needn't worry any more."

"Why?" asked the forlorn lunatic, eagerly.

"Because he's dead again."

"Dead! Dead! Oh, don't trifle with a poor wreck like me. Is he dead? On honor, now — is he telling me true, boys?"

"True as you're standing there!" said Ham Sandwich, and they all backed up the statement in a body.

"They hung him in San Bernardino last week," added Ferguson, clinching the matter, "whilst he was searching around after you. Mistook him for another man. They're sorry, but they can't help it now."

"They're a-building him a monument," said Ham Sandwich, with the air of a person who had contributed to it, and knew.

"James Walker" drew a deep sigh — evidently a sigh of relief — and said nothing; but his eyes lost something of their wildness, his countenance cleared visibly, and its drawn look relaxed a little. We all went to our cabin, and the boys cooked him the best dinner the camp could furnish the materials for, and while they were about it Hillyer and I outfitted him from hat to shoe-leather with new clothes of ours, and made a comely and presentable old gentleman of him. "Old" is the right word, and a pity, too; old by the droop of him, and the frost upon his hair, and the marks which sorrow and distress have left upon his face; though he is only in his prime in the matter of years. While he ate, we smoked and chatted; and when he was finishing he found his voice at last, and of his own accord broke out with his personal history. I cannot furnish his exact words, but I will come as near it as I can.

THE "WRONG MAN'S" STORY

It happened like this: I was in Denver. I had been there many years; sometimes I remember how many, sometimes I don't — but it isn't any matter. All of a sudden I got a notice to leave, or I would be exposed for a horrible crime committed long before — years and years before — in the East.

I knew about that crime, but I was not the criminal; it was a cousin of mine of the same name. What should I better do? My head was all disordered by fear, and I didn't know. I was allowed very little time — only one day, I think it was. I would be ruined if I was published, and the people would lynch me, and not believe what I said. It is always the way with lynchings: when they find out it is a mistake they are sorry, but it is too late — the same as it was with Mr. Holmes, you see. So I said I would sell out and get money to live on, and run away until it blew over and I could come back with my proofs. Then I escaped in the night and went a long way off in the mountains somewhere, and lived disguised and had a false name.

I got more and more troubled and worried, and my troubles

made me see spirits and hear voices, and I could not think straight and clear on any subject, but got confused and involved and had to give it up, because my head hurt so. It got to be worse and worse; more spirits and more voices. They were about me all the time; at first only in the night, then in the day too. They were always whispering around my bed and plotting against me, and it broke my sleep and kept me fagged out, because I got no good rest.

And then came the worst. One night the whispers said, "We'll never manage, because we can't see him, and so can't point him out to the people."

They sighed; then one said: "We must bring Sherlock Holmes. He can be here in twelve days."

They all agreed, and whispered and jibbered with joy. But my heart broke; for I had read about that man, and knew what it would be to have him upon my track, with his superhuman penetration and tireless energies.

The spirits went away to fetch him, and I got up at once in the middle of the night and fled away, carrying nothing but the hand-bag that had my money in it — thirty thousand dollars; two-thirds of it are in the bag there yet. It was forty days before that man caught up on my track. I just escaped. From habit he had written his real name on a tavern register, but had scratched it out and written "Dagget Barclay" in the place of it. But fear gives you a watchful eye and keen, and I read the true name through the scratches, and fled like a deer.

He has hunted me all over this world for three years and a half — the Pacific states, Australasia, India — everywhere you can think of; then back to Mexico and up to California again, giving me hardly any rest; but that name on the registers always saved me, and what is left of me is alive yet. And I am so tired! A cruel time he has given me, yet I give you my honor I have never harmed him nor any man.

That was the end of the story, and it stirred those boys to blood-heat, be sure of it. As for me — each word burnt a hole in me where it struck.

We voted that the old man should bunk with us, and be my guest and Hillyer's. I shall keep my own counsel, naturally; but as soon as he is well rested and nourished, I shall take him to Denver and rehabilitate his fortunes.

The boys gave the old fellow the bone-mashing good-fellowship handshake of the mines, and then scattered away to spread the news.

At dawn next morning Wells-Fargo Ferguson and Ham Sandwich called us softly out, and said, privately,

"That news about the way that old stranger has been treated has spread all around, and the camps are up. They are piling in from everywhere, and are going to lynch the P'fessor. Constable Harris is in a dead funk, and has telephoned the sheriff. Come along!"

We started on a run. The others were privileged to feel as they chose, but in my heart's privacy I hoped the sheriff would arrive in time; for I had small desire that Sherlock Holmes should hang for my deeds, as you can easily believe. I had heard a good deal about the sheriff, but for reassurance's sake I asked,

"Can he stop a mob?"

"Can he stop a mob! Can Jack Fairfax stop a mob! Well, I should smile! Ex-desperado — nineteen scalps on his string. Can he! Oh, I say!"

As we tore up the gulch, distant cries and shouts and yells

rose faintly on the still air, and grew steadily in strength as we raced along. Roar after roar burst out, stronger and stronger, nearer and nearer; and at last, when we closed up upon the multitude massed in the open area in front of the tavern, the crash of sound was deafening. Some brutal roughs from Daly's gorge had Holmes in their grip, and he was the calmest man there; a contemptuous smile played about his lips, and if any fear of death was in his British heart, his iron personality was master of it and no sign of it was allowed to appear.

"Come to a vote, men!" This from one of the Daly gang, Shadbelly Higgins. "Quick! is it hang, or shoot?"

"Neither!" shouted one of his comrades. "He'll be alive again in a week; burning's the only permanency for him."

The gangs from all the outlying camps burst out in a thunder-crash of approval, and went struggling and surging toward the prisoner, and closed around him, shouting, "Fire! Fire's the ticket!" They dragged him to the horse-post, backed him against it, chained him to it, and piled wood and pine cones around him waist-deep. Still the strong face did not blench, and still the scornful smile played about the thin lips.

"A match! fetch a match!"

Shadbelly struck it, shaded it with his hand, stooped, and held it under a pine cone. A deep silence fell upon the mob. The cone caught, a tiny flame flickered about it a moment or two. I seemed to catch the sound of distant hoofs — it grew more distinct — still more and more distinct, more and more definite, but the absorbed crowd did not appear to notice it. The match went out. The man struck another, stooped, and again the flame rose; this time it took hold and began to spread — here and there men turned away their faces. The executioner stood with the charred match in his fingers, watching his work. The hoof-beats turned a projecting crag, and now they came thundering down upon us. Almost the next moment there was a shout —

"The sheriff!"

And straightway he came tearing into the midst, stood his horse almost on his hind feet, and said,

"Fall back, you gutter-snipes!"

He was obeyed. By all but their leader. He stood his ground, and his hand went to his revolver. The sheriff covered him promptly, and said,

"Drop your hand, you parlor-desperado. Kick the fire away. Now unchain the stranger."

The parlor-desperado obeyed. Then the sheriff made a speech; sitting his horse at martial ease, and not warming his words with any touch of fire, but delivering them in a measured and deliberate way, and in a tone which harmonized with their character and made them impressively disrespectful.

"You're a nice lot — now ain't you? Just about eligible to travel with this bilk here — Shadbelly Higgins — this loud-mouthed sneak that shoots people in the back and calls himself a desperado. If there's anything I do particularly despise, it's a lynching mob; I've never seen one that had a man in it. It has to tally up a hundred against one before it can pump up pluck enough to tackle a sick tailor. It's made up of cowards, and so is the community that breeds it; and ninety-nine times out of a hundred the sheriff's another one." He paused — apparently to turn that last idea over in his mind and taste the juice of it — then he went on: "The sheriff that lets a mob take a prisoner away from him is the lowest-down coward there is. By the statistics there was a hundred and eighty-two of them drawing

sneak pay in America last year. By the way it's going, pretty soon
there'll be a new disease in the doctor-books — sheriff complaint."
That idea pleased him — any one could see it. "People will say,
'Sheriff sick again?' 'Yes; got the same old thing.' And next
there'll be a new title. People won't say, 'He's running for sheriff
of Rapaho County,' for instance; they'll say, 'He's running for
Coward of Rapaho.' Lord, the idea of a grown-up person being
afraid of a lynch mob!"

He turned an eye on the captive, and said, "Stranger, who are
you, and what have you been doing?"

"My name is Sherlock Holmes, and I have not been doing
anything."

It was wonderful, the impression which the sound of that
name made on the sheriff, notwithstanding he must have come
posted. He spoke up with feeling, and said it was a blot on the
country that a man whose marvelous exploits had filled the
world with their fame and their ingenuity, and whose histories
of them had won every reader's heart by the brilliancy and
charm of their literary setting, should be visited under the Stars
and Stripes by an outrage like this. He apologized in the name
of the whole nation, and made Holmes a most handsome bow,
and told Constable Harris to see him to his quarters, and hold
himself personally responsible if he was molested again. Then
he turned to the mob and said,

"Hunt your holes, you scum!" which they did; then he said:
"Follow me, Shadbelly; I'll take care of your case myself. No —
keep your pop-gun; whenever I see the day that I'll be afraid to
have you behind me with that thing, it'll be time for me to join
last year's hundred and eighty-two"; and he rode off in a walk,
Shadbelly following.

When we were on our way back to our cabin, toward breakfast-time, we ran upon the news that Fetlock Jones had escaped from his lock-up in the night and is gone! Nobody is sorry. Let his uncle track him out if he likes; it is in his line; the camp is not interested.

V

TEN DAYS LATER —

"James Walker" is all right in body now, and his mind shows improvement too. I start with him for Denver to-morrow morning.

Next night. Brief note, mailed at a waystation —

As we were starting, this morning, Hillyer whispered to me: "Keep this news from Walker until you think it safe and not likely to disturb his mind and check his improvement: the ancient crime he spoke of was really committed — and by his cousin, as he said. We buried the real criminal the other day — the unhappiest man that has lived in a century — Flint Buckner. His real name was Jacob Fuller!" There, mother, by help of me, an unwitting mourner, your husband and my father is in his grave. Let him rest.